Quest for the Midas Orb

Mark Anderson

Contents

Foreword

In a window above the blacksmith's shop could be seen the silhouette of a woman. The woman was rubbing her body down with some oils from an urn. Across the road was a bank. As one person left, several others entered. There were two horses tied up outside the telegraph store, and several woman and children were on their way back from the temple. To the north of town could be seen a herd of cattle and to the west a herd of goats. One man tended the goats as his dog pushed them homeward. In the general store were two women buying flour. A man behind them had a small bucket and shovel in his hand, and another had a sack of corn and some cigars.

Inside the tavern, Javan was belly up to the bar talking to a friend, enjoying the midday conversation, when a short man walked into the tavern. He asked the piano player for directions and, after being pointed towards Javan, headed over to his stool. The man handed Javan a small rolled-up piece of linen, turned, and quickly left. Javan glanced at his friend and smirked. He was not quite sure what to think but opened up the scroll and read what was inside:

"Meet me at Dugan's Stables at sunrise tomorrow morning. I have important travels ahead and need your help. Joshua."

Javan knew of this man Joshua but was not familiar with his travels. The two men went back to talking and ordered another drink from the bartender. Meanwhile, one of the tavern patrons in the back of the bar decided to get frisky with one of the female waitresses and was thrown through a side window in a splattering of broken glass. A slight melee ensued. Javan, a sturdy fighter, stood up, all six feet and five inches of him intimidating some of the patrons. He started towards the melee when the bartender stopped him. Javan stopped and let the bartender pass. The bartender quickly quieted the rowdy bunch and showed several of the guests out of the tavern. He returned behind the bar and finished washing his glassware. Javan turned back to the bar, slammed down another tub of ale, said goodbye to his friend, and left the tavern.

Lucas was in the middle of some early evening fun with a female guest when there was a loud knock at the door! Lucas shook his head, rose from the bed, and pulled up his pants. Lucas was a muscular man with the arms of a skilled sword fighter who stood six feet tall.

The woman, naked, got out of bed and walked to the wardrobe to grab a nightgown. She returned wearing a red nightgown that was falling off her shoulders. She turned to go answer the door when Lucas stopped her and went to the door himself. On the other side of the door was a small man, not more than five feet tall, carrying a small piece of rolled up linen. He handed Lucas a scroll and darted away. Lucas shut the door and brought the scroll back into his bedroom and unrolled it. He read aloud the message inside:

"Meet me at Dugan's Stables at sunrise tomorrow morning. I have important travels ahead and need your help. Joshua."

Lucas grumbled under his breath and glanced at the woman. He pulled his pants back off of him and crawled back into bed. The woman, in her mid-twenties, let the nightgown fall from her shoulders and got into bed next to him. Lucas grabbed her and pulled her towards him. Lucas thought about Joshua and what adventure was coming that he needed his help. He kissed her again, hoping it would not be the last time. Paleo was busy working in the stables repairing a piece of broken fencing when someone called to him.

"Are you Paleo?" the voice asked.

He turned around and answered. The man, no taller than a small pony, handed Paleo a small piece of paper rolled up into a scroll. The man bowed his head and quickly scurried away. Paleo took the scroll but put it aside to finish his chores. After feeding the horses, tending to the hogs, and letting the dogs out for a midday run, Paleo sat down to read the scroll:

"Meet me at Dugan's Stables at sunrise tomorrow morning. I have important travels ahead and need your help. Joshua."

Paleo put his hand on his chin and rubbed it, looking for an answer to who this man was.

Joshua? he thought. *I bet the man I met last week at the temple. Must be important,* he thought and returned to finish his chores.

A small man opened the doors to the Druidanis temple, peered inside, and walked in. He looked around to see if anyone was there. Seeing no one, he walked towards the altar when suddenly a voice called out.

"Come here, my child. Let me help you with your troubles."

Startled, the man dropped the scroll he was carrying, turned, and ran out the door. From the shadows came a frail-looking man. He wore a dark robe and well-worn sandals. He picked up the scroll and examined it carefully. Not recognizing the seal, he broke it open and read it:

"Meet me at Dugan's Stables at sunrise tomorrow morning. I have important travels ahead and need your help. Joshua."

Aran did not know any person named Joshua but was always up for a good adventure, so he decided that this must have been meant for him and he would be there to meet with this person called Joshua. Aran returned to the shadows, chanting as he disappeared out of sight.

He had spent months behind bars. He had spent months doing hard time. Now he was only a few feet away from being free when suddenly someone came into the building! Segor crawled out from under his bed, threw his cloak on, and waited on the bed. He looked up to see a small man, maybe five feet tall, holding a small piece of paper. The man was at his jail cell and handed the scroll to Segor. After giving Segor the scroll, the man fled out the door and down the road into the wilderness. Segor, seemed puzzled by the man's strange gift but nonetheless opened it up and read the inscription:

"Meet me at Dugan's Stables at sunrise tomorrow morning. I have important travels ahead and need your help. Joshua."

5

Segor remembered meeting a Joshua once in another land, but he was sure this couldn't be the same guy! After resting for a few more moments, Segor returned to the hole under his cot and continued his digging. Several minutes later, he broke through the ground, coming up behind the armory. He covered the opening with branches and pulled himself back into his cell. He would wait there until nightfall and then escape. He had waited so long, and now he would finally be free!

Joshua was sitting at his table eating, when a stranger knocked on the door. He got up, answered the door, and found a small man outside.

"All the scrolls have been delivered, master," pronounced the man and held out his hand.

"Thank you," replied Joshua, giving the man three gold pieces.

The man bowed his head, turned around, and hurried down the lane. Joshua returned to his table and sat down again. A woman brought him another bowl of broth. Joshua finished it and retired to the bedroom where his female guest was waiting for him. She was lying in bed, and Joshua crawled in next to her.

He pulled the woman close and whispered in her ear, "This may be the last night we spend together."

She replied, "I know."

She leaned over and kissed him. Joshua kissed her back, pulled her gown off her, and threw it onto the floor. He rolled her over so that he was on top of her and started kissing her from her neck down to her stomach.

Night began to fall upon the small town as several horsemen rode in and stopped at the tavern. The three men went into the tavern. Two women wandered past outside and headed for the general store, just a few buildings away. Someone was playing music in a room above the post office, and another was sitting on the porch, strumming a guitar and humming along. All seemed well, and another hot, dry day was just about over. For most it meant time to rest. Suddenly, from behind the armory came some movement. A dark, shadowy figure pulled itself out of a hole in the ground and freed itself from months of incarceration and slipped away into the night! In the distance, a wolf howled, and a rabbit could be seen scurrying across the road. Lightning bugs filled the skies, giving the city a bright glow as night fell upon it.

Chapter 1

The skies were covered with clouds, and the temperature was especially cool this night. Distant lightning could be seen, and thunder rumbled through the heavens. The howling of wolves and the crackling of a small campfire broke the eeriness of the night. The last of the flames were sizzling out when the skies broke loose in a fury of sleet and rain. The fire was quickly doused, and the six men were drenched. With their clothes and equipment soaked, they decided to trudge on through the night. Up ahead, they knew, was a cave, a haven for weary travelers caught in their unfriendly surroundings.

After several hours of stumbling through the forest, they came upon the cave. By now, the storm had subsided and the wolves' faint howls had all but vanished. The men hungrily ran to the cave entrance but entered with grave caution. They didn't want to walk into any sleeping animals, most of all, any waiting dragons.

One of the men entered first.

"Everyone be careful while Lucas and I examine the cave. We may have to take it over first," said the man entering the mouth of the cave.

Lucas and Javan went in and quickly searched the cave for any sleeping animals or, if they were lucky enough, any treasure. After finding neither, they returned to the opening of the cave and motioned for everyone else to enter. The men entered and made themselves as comfortable as possible and went to sleep for the rest of the night. It had been a long four days on the road, and they had a long way yet to go.

When the men awoke in the morning, they quickly learned that three brown bears had entered the cave overnight and fallen asleep right next to Javan! Lucas and Segor decided to gather up all of their belongings and get the rest of the group out of the cave. Segor would then go back in and awake Javan but hopefully not the bears!

After everyone had left the cave and was hidden outside, Segor crept back into the cave and over to Javan. He was beginning to stir!

"Javan, don't move. Please don't move," whispered Segor, holding Javan down.

"What?" stuttered Javan.

"Shhh! You are lying next to three brown bears! Don't move."

Javan quickly tensed up and froze.

Segor helped Javan to his feet and helped him carry his things out of the cave. They had just reached the opening when they heard a loud growl. Fearing the bears were right behind them, they threw their stuff aside and dove into the bushes surrounding the cave entrance. Not more than five seconds later, the bears came running out of the cave and headed into the wilderness, just missing Segor and Javan! A bit shaken from the close encounter, Javan suggested everyone gather their things and make their way to the castle as soon as possible.

Chapter 2

Under a light blue sky scattered with white puffy clouds, the men trudged on to the north. Through tall grass and brush, they walked without any further encounters. Now and then, one would run into a snake or a small animal but nothing they couldn't handle. Suddenly, Javan raised his left hand, and the group scattered into the brush, drawing their weapons. Ahead they could see three large human-like creatures, Ogres. They were headed right toward the men, and each one carried a sack and a battle axe! The Ogres grumbled and snorted as they walked on.

The Ogres were still several yards away when Joshua fired his bow. Four of the six arrows he fired hit their mark, and one of the Ogres fell. Startled by the quick dropping of their pal, the other two Ogres dropped their sacks and grabbed their battle axes, ready for action.

Javan and then Lucas ran forward with their weapons and attacked the remaining Ogres. The Ogre that had fallen to the ground got back up, managing to avoid a slash from Joshua. The Ogre, in turn, tried to hit Joshua but also missed. Joshua's second swing caught the bewildered Ogre in the chest, and again he fell to the ground, hitting it like a fallen tree. With blood covering his sword, Joshua turned around to see Lucas get hit in the arm by a blow from one of the Ogre's axes.

Segor and Aran had taken time to sneak up from behind, and with a signal from Segor, they attacked the backs of the Ogres ferociously. With blood squirting, both Ogres fell to the ground and died.

The men were a little tired but were nonetheless glad that it hadn't taken long for them to defeat the Ogres. Aran took out some bandages and quickly bandaged Lucas's arm. Segor and Javan began opening up the Ogres' sacks to see what was inside of them. Segor found dead animals and several copper coins in one sack. Javan found only dried fruits and several gold coins in another. Javan collected the coins and put them into his shoulder sack. The third and final sack had fruits and vegetables in it, so they threw it aside and made sure everyone else was okay. The men gathered up again and proceeded along through the brush and shrubs for another three or four hours until they decided to stop and rest.

There wasn't a cloud in the sky, and the air smelled fresh and clean, making their journey a little easier. As the day went along, the sun made the air hotter and hotter, so the men stopped frequently to catch their breaths and get a drink of water to cool off.

At midday, Javan noticed an object in the distance.

"I think that's the castle ahead, but it is probably five or six hours off yet."

"We should make it by sundown," said Paleo, "but may I suggest we camp outside tonight and enter the castle tomorrow?"

They all agreed that would be best. With water supplies running low and everyone anticipating tomorrow's adventure into the castle, the rest of the trip to the castle seemed to take forever. Finally they made it and felt relieved, to say the least, that they were all still in one piece.

When they got close enough to see the castle, they noticed it was surrounded by a large, deep moat; however, the drawbridge was currently down! They all looked at each other in surprise.

The front façade of the castle looked like some sort of bull with the mouth as the opening. The rest of its head was formed above the door, forbidding anyone to enter. There were two windows, one on each side of the entrance. The windows were shaped into the form of cat's claws, with the claws forming the bars over the windows. The castle had two tall lookout towers, one to the east and the other to the west.

"Let's search the area and see if there is a place to sleep tonight," suggested Javan. "We will have to keep watch, so let's draw grasses for the first, second, and third watch, okay?"

After searching the area around the entrance to the castle and finding a place to bed down, Javan cut off some grasses and gave them to Paleo to hold. Javan then drew first—three inches long. Next to draw was Lucas—four inches long. Joshua drew three and a half inches long. Next was Aran, and he drew a grass three inches long. Segor quickly pulled out one of the last two grasses—two and a half inches long. Paleo measured his and found it to be four inches long. Segor would take the first watch, Javan the second, and Aran the third watch of the night. Segor searched for a good place for a post while the others made camp and hurried to sleep.

Chapter 3

The night went by rather slowly for Segor, but with a cool breeze and the chirping of the crickets, he had no trouble staying awake. Every now and then an owl would startle him or a bat would fly overhead, but he kept his cool and managed to keep his wits. After watching the stars and moon drift slowly by, he decided it was time for someone else to take watch. He climbed down out of the tree he was in and walked over to where the others were sleeping. Without even seeing the empty sleeping bag, Segor could sense something was wrong! He quickly woke Javan and Lucas and was waking up Joshua and Aran when Javan decided that they search the area for their missing friend.

"Joshua and Lucas, start to the right, go out about fifty yards, and circle around. Aran and Segor and I will go to the left and do the same," directed Javan. "Look for anything unusual. Any little sign could save his life!"

Each group lit a torch and took off.

The area was covered with thick thorns and brush. The wind had picked up, slowing down their searching efforts. After several hours of searching for any clue to Paleo's whereabouts proved fruitless, they gathered again by camp. The sun was on its way up, and day was breaking. Discouraged and bewildered, they decided to continue on into the castle; perhaps they would find him inside, waiting for them.

Javan and Lucas took to the point and led the group into the castle. The drawbridge was still down, so they proceeded to the entrance. The doors to the castle were heavy wooden doors bound with brass bands. Javan and Lucas pushed the doors open with very little effort. The rest stood with weapons ready. It was dark inside, so they had to light a torch. Aran agreed to carry it.

After they checked their weapons and took a collective deep breath, they went on. As they walked into the castle, they entered a rather well-kept courtyard. The ground was dirt, and there were several stone planters that contained clusters of trees, bushes, and plants. Some weeds had started taking over the gardens, but everything seemed to be in place. Javan and Segor took a better look around, while the rest searched the entrance. Javan and Segor found several broken twigs and branches throughout the courtyard but nothing else. Javan also noticed several places in the dirt that were damp. There were some footprints in the dirt, but Javan didn't recognize them. Javan wondered if they could have been Paleo's, but he didn't know for sure.

After telling everyone of their findings, Javan and Segor searched the walls of the courtyard. The courtyard walls were made of gray stone. They noticed the south wall of the courtyard was only ten feet high; however, each of the other walls was over twenty feet high.

After several minutes of searching revealed nothing, the men decided to continue farther into the castle. Two more heavy wooden doors with brass bands were set into the north wall, so that was the way they went. Again the doors pushed open rather easily, and the men entered a chamber. Just as the last man entered the chamber, the doors slammed shut behind them with a loud bang!

They also heard a loud click as if it had been locked. Joshua tried to push it open again, but no matter how hard he pushed or how many of them pushed or pulled, it did not open. They had been locked in!

"It looks as though we have to continue on now," said Javan after realizing the doors were not going to open again.

Proceeding with extreme caution, Javan and Lucas, still leading the group, peered behind the draperies flanking the long corridor. The drapery on the west wall had nothing behind it. The drapery on the east wall, however, covered up a small alcove that contained a peg with a cloak hanging from it.

"Segor, keep guard while the rest of us check this out," directed Javan, pointing to a place outside the alcove for him to stand.

"Alright," he replied and took stand.

Aran, Joshua, Lucas, and Javan entered the alcove and lifted the cloak off of the peg. Aran examined the cloak carefully while the rest looked for hidden doors. Aran found a small secret pocket in the cloak. Avoiding notice by the others, Aran took out what was inside the pocket and slipped the platinum pieces into his pouch belt.

Javan happened to turn around and see Aran slip the coins into his pouch belt and said, "Nothing of value in the cloak, huh?"

Bewildered but trying hard to cover it up, Aran said in reply, "No, there was nothing on the cloak."

He then threw the cloak to the ground and joined the rest of the men.

They all left the alcove and rejoined Segor outside. He had a horrified look upon his face!

"Segor, what is wrong?" demanded Lucas, who looked around to see if he could figure out what had Segor so shocked.

"I...I...I..." stuttered Segor.

"What?" asked Javan, getting ready to slap Segor if he needed it.

"I saw two flashes of light in the room ahead! They were red and fiery-looking!"

"You got to be kidding! Why, then, didn't you say something?"

"B-because," Segor stuttered. "I wasn't sure if it was really what I saw. I was just turning around when I saw the flashes of light." Segor's face had quickly turned into thought as if he was thinking of what he had really seen.

"Well, we'd better go and see if we can find anything in there."

Javan took the lead.

Advancing as quietly as possible with heavy armor on, the men entered the chamber. Segor smirked, seeing how frightened the rest of the group seemed to be. Several glowing discs already lighted the chamber, one on each side of the chamber and two in each corner. The floor was made of a highly polished marble.

As the men went farther into the chamber, they could see a gold vein running through the floor. As they looked around, they could see five large tapestries depicting various knights doing heroic deeds hanging from the walls.

Javan examined one of the tapestries and noticed it was made of wool and of really good workmanship, but there was not worth much to them since they were here for a different purpose. The chamber had six archways in it, so they voted to see which one they'd take first. After deciding on the one to the immediate right, they headed down the corridor.

That corridor had rust-colored tiles lining the walls. The floor was made of moss-green flagstone, which made each step they took echo louder and louder. After several more steps, they could hear other sounds. They seemed to be heading right towards them!

"There are others coming towards us!" exclaimed Javan. "Draw your weapons and get ready!"

Within seconds, they could see two boogerbears heading right toward them. Each boogerbear carried a long sword and wore a suit of banded armor.

Defending himself well, Javan avoided being hit by the one of boogerbears. Also up front with Javan was Lucas. He covered his bandaged arm with his shield and struck wildly at first and then with much more skill at another of the boogerbears. They forced the boogerbears backwards and allowed Aran to get into the fight.

Aran swung his club and caught Lucas in the side, throwing him forward. The boogerbear saw his chance and attacked, hitting Lucas in the back. The force of the blow threw Lucas down. The boogerbear was upon Lucas and attacked him again. Aran stayed in his position and got in a good shot to the other boogerbear, hitting him and throwing him back several feet. The boogerbears sword went flying and almost hit the other boogerbear in the process. Javan, angry over the carelessness that could have killed Lucas, gathered up all his might and took a long, wide swing that completely chopped the head off one of the boogerbears. Falling to the floor, the boogerbear squirted blood everywhere. Moments later, the second boogerbear fell to the ground dead! With blood dripping from his sword, Javan turned toward Aran and started yelling at him.

"What in the hell do you think you are doing? Trying to kill our own party members or what? Goddamn it! Would you please be more careful next time, Aran?"

Aran stared at Javan and yelled back, "It was a bad break, that's all! Sorry!"

Joshua ran forward to help Lucas but accidentally bumped into Aran as he went by him.

"Watch out, you damn fool," he yelled at Joshua.

"Hey!" shouted Javan. "We don't need any hostility amongst ourselves. Try and have some patience, okay, Aran?"

"Fine, but it's not just me."

"Joshua?" asked Javan.

"Oh, alright, just watch your swing next time," Joshua replied as reached Lucas.

Segor and Joshua, thinking about the mysterious disappearance of Paleo, quickly helped Lucas to his feet so they wouldn't lose him, too!

Segor helped Lucas along as the men walked down the corridor and entered another chamber ahead of them. They found themselves in what looked like a trophy room.

Taking up the entire south wall was a hanging made from the skin of a red dragon. Elsewhere in the room was a huge stuffed white bear, a pair of stuffed badgers, a stuffed giant eagle, a stuffed wild boar, and two stuffed giant rams.

Javan and Aran went over to examine the red dragon skin while the rest started investigating the rest of the room's contents. Javan and Aran attempted to lift the red dragon skin off of the wall. As they did so, they heard several loud screams from behind them. They quickly spun around to see Lucas and Joshua being bucked backwards by two now-animated giant rams!

Javan ran up and drew his sword, followed by Aran and then Segor. The giant rams quickly trampled Lucas and Joshua before any of the others could get to help them out. Javan got in several good shots on the rams but not before Lucas and Joshua lay on the ground bleeding from the attacks. The giant rams turned and started bucking at Javan and the others. The men retreated and led the rams away from the two hurt men lying on the ground. They beat each ram again with their weapons.

The giant rams' white fur coats were turning red as Javan and the others did as much damage to them as they could. One ram bucked Aran down and then turned and bucked Javan. Javan went flying headlong and was bucked by the second giant ram, who sent him backwards and to the ground. Javan lay on the ground in a bruised heap. Segor, alone at the time, shot his dagger right into the head of one of the giant rams. The ram stopped cold in its tracks and hit the ground hard. Blood gushed from its head. By now, Aran had recovered, stood back up, and struck with three good whacks of his mace. The blows sent the second giant ram crashing to the floor. Aran had broken its back, and it was dead!

Joshua and Lucas lay on the floor in the center of the room, so Javan, Aran, and Segor ran to their assistance. Aran used his last bandages for Joshua and Segor, and Javan bandaged Lucas for the third time. After a few minutes to rest and gain their composure, Javan decided it would be a good idea to get rid of any more chances of animated attacks, so he sliced in half the rest of the stuffed animals in the room.

Noticing that Lucas and Joshua had regained their strength, Aran and Javan again tried to lift the red dragon skin from the wall. This time they removed it, put it down on the floor, and discovered a small niche behind the skin. Javan reached in and pulled out a small velvet pouch. He carefully opened it. Inside were two sparkling diamonds. They were quite large and most likely worth a great deal. He put them back into the pouch and placed the pouch into his shoulder sack. They would divide everything found after the adventure was over.

The men picked up everything they'd dropped in the fight and headed back out into the large chamber. Lucas was on Aran's arm, and Joshua used Segor as a support. Battered and worn out, they made it back into the chamber of archways and rested. Here they decided to turn in for the night. It was obvious any creature entering the chamber would be heard, so they didn't have to guard against any intruders that night. The night went by without any problems.

Chapter 4

The town of Gnarda was a buzz as the sun came up for another day. Three women ran to the sheriff's office and burst in. Several men came out of the telegraph office and ran over to the blacksmith's shop. From the outskirts of town came three men riding horses. They stopped at the sheriff's office and went in. Across town, in one of the townsfolk's homes could be seen a woman bending over a figure lying on the ground. Surrounding the body was a puddle of blood and several pieces of wood. The woman was crying and tried feverishly to revive the person lying motionless. Off in the distance stood a castle...

The five men awoke in the morning, refreshed and ready to go. They gathered their belongings and entered the corridor on the northeast side of the chamber.

This corridor was tiled in magenta and didn't seem to be as loud as the last one they were in. At the end of the thirty-foot corridor was a door. The door was not locked and opened very easily into what appeared to be a music room.

The room had a number of finely made instruments in it. All of them were in pristine condition and seemed to be playable. The instruments were in an alcove carved out of the rock wall: a lute, three harps, a mandolin, and a bandore. After carefully examining each instrument, they decided to leave the room as there was nothing there of importance. Again they went back into the arched chamber.

"We need to keep going," said Joshua, leading the group deeper into the castle. Back in the great chamber, they went to the opposite side they had before in hopes of finding something of value there. The men entered an archway in the southwest corner. This corridor was flame-colored and looked more like the surrounding chamber walls. It also had a dirt floor.

Coming up to a corner, Segor took off in front and quietly but cautiously rounded it. He told the rest to wait for his signal.

They waited.

After several minutes and no signal from Segor, they decided to go on anyway. When they turned the corner, they saw a set of steps that descended at least a full floor down. When they got to the bottom of the steps, the corridor turned again and opened into another chamber.

When they entered the chamber, they saw Segor several steps up a raised platform. As they approached, they could hear moans coming from the platform. When Segor saw them approaching, he motioned for them to come closer. Atop the platform was a pit. Javan, Lucas, and Aran ascended. As Joshua stepped up to the final step, he tripped and went sprawling right toward the pit! Acting upon a quick impulse, Lucas reached out and grabbed Joshua, stopping him only inches from the pit's edge. Joshua lay on the ground for a while to catch his breath. When he realized what had happened, he thanked Lucas for saving him.

"You're welcome, pal," replied Lucas, patting Joshua on the back.

Segor explained that he had walked the distance of the corridor and entered the chamber. He had found nothing and was about to call for the rest when he heard the moans coming from the pit. He was in the process of finding out what was in the pit when they entered.

Upon exploring the pit closer, they could see a ladder had been spiked to the ground and dangled down into the pit. Segor was about ready to climb down into the pit and check it out when he noticed the pit had very smooth walls.

"Wait! Let's drop a torch into it and see how deep it goes," said Javan, who lit another torch with his flint box.

He reached the torch over the edge of the pit and let it go. The torch fell for several seconds before it suddenly went out. The men were astonished! They heard a faint splash and fizzle as the torch light went out.

"Sounds like there is water down there," said Aran.

"I'm going down to see what I can find," replied Segor. "I'm the only one light enough to make it, and besides, I'm awfully curious."

"Wait, tie a rope around your waist so that if the ladder breaks, you won't fall all the way down with no way back up," said Javan, who turned and took off his backpack. He pulled out a rope.

"Good idea!"

They tied one end of the rope around Segor's waist and waited apprehensively for Segor to descend. When the rope was secure and Segor was ready, he descended. He took each rung of the ladder with caution. He had gone about thirty feet when he came to last rung of the ladder. That was not, however, the bottom of the pit. Segor looked around for something, anything of importance, but found nothing. He yelled up for Javan and Joshua to pull him up, and within a couple of seconds, he was out of the pit again.

"I couldn't reach the bottom and didn't see anything that might help us," reported Segor. He untied the rope from his waist.

"Let's keep going," said Javan as he put the rope back into his backpack.

There was a passage branching off the chamber in the northeast corner, so they decided to see what lay beyond it. To their left and also ahead of them were what appeared to be prison cells. In the cell to their left was a hideous creature with one sensory organ and two tentacles. The cell was filled with offal and smelt of urine and decay.

Segor winced at the sight and moved to the back of the passage, working his way to the back of the group. As the rest moved ahead past the cell, he took out his lock pick set and picked the lock on the door to the cell with the hideous creature in it. He pushed the door open slightly and ran back into the chamber they all had just come from.

He had waited a long time for this chance to betray the group, and now the time had come. As he headed for the main chamber in the castle, he suddenly stopped dead in his tracks—there was a loud, ear-piercing scream! He looked back to make sure nothing was following him, grinned, and continued on. He went back through the courtyard and left the castle running as fast as he could.

Joshua and Lucas were grabbed from behind by the dung-eating creature's tentacles and thrown to the ground. They screamed as loud as they could! Aran and Javan whirled around, expecting the worst. They got it! Javan could see that Joshua and Lucas were being suffocated by the creature, so he grabbed his sword and advanced to attack. As he neared, the hideous odor of the creature hit him. It was the worst odor he had ever smelt, and it made him weak and nauseated. He choked and threw up. He couldn't go any further. He had to turn and back away. Aran tried to advance also, but he, too, found the odor too much for him to handle. Aran dropped to the ground and covered his face. His eyes began to water from the stench! Javan, although completely grossed out from the stench, could still move, so he did. Quickly he slashed at the creature and gashed him in four places. One slash completely chopped off a tentacle! As the creature reeled from the attack, Javan reached back with all his might and once again with a mighty blow gashed open its fleshy body. The creature was stunned for a second, which allowed Javan several more skilled attacks. The creature's body slumped to the ground, completely covering Joshua and Lucas. Aran was still on the ground reeling from the stench, so Javan took what he could of a deep breath of air and thrust himself into the creature's body, finally pushing it off his friends.

He hoped he was not too late! Had his friends been suffocated by the weight of the grotesque creature? He would soon find out. He pulled them both to safety and quickly tried to revive them both. After what seemed like an eternity, they started to stir and opened their eyes, gasping for air. Javan took a deep breath and collapsed to the ground exhausted. They would be alright this time.

Several minutes later, Javan regained his strength and helped a bloody Lucas to the outside chamber as Joshua stumbled behind them. Aran walked out seconds later and helped attend to Lucas's needs. It took several minutes more before Javan realized Segor was gone.

"Hey, where the hell is Segor?" he asked, frantically searching for him.

They all looked around for Segor.

"I don't know," responded Aran. "Maybe he got hit by the creature, too.

"No, I didn't see him even in the fight!" exclaimed Javan. "Where the hell is he?"

"I don't know, man," stated Joshua, still coughing and gasping for fresh air.

"He had better not be responsible for this attack on us," stated Javan. "But I swear, that cell door was closed when we walked past it. How could that thing have gotten out if not for him?"

Javan threw his sword down in disgust.

"Fuck!" he screamed. "I had not better see him again, or I will kill him with my own bare hands!" Javan spit onto the ground.

Javan continued to curse Segor as he walked back into the passage and past the dead creature. He walked up to the next cell and peered in. Javan saw an enraged creature inside. It was thrashing and beating the door with a dreadful noise. It was an eight-foot-tall humanoid creature with the head of a bull. Javan knew what it was and decided to leave immediately before he had to deal with the Minotaur, too.

Javan walked back past the dead creature and cursed it as he did so, spitting on its grotesque, lifeless body. He entered the outside chamber again and found everyone still groggy from the ordeal. They rested a little longer and then went back to the huge ballroom chamber again.

They all were feeling drained and tired, so they decided get some rest for the night in the ballroom. Javan would take watch for a while, and then Aran would take his turn.

Chapter 5

Several men had gathered at the armory and seemed to be waiting for someone. One man whittled on a piece of wood while another smoked a cigarette. The puffs of smoke rose into the night sky like little smoke signals from some distant Indian tribe fire. The men had been waiting about half an hour when someone in a long, black cloak walked up from behind a nearby building. All the men greeted him. The cloaked figure went on to speak.

"Thank you all for showing up tonight. I know by your loyalty to me tonight that I can trust each and every one of you," the figure went on. "I have big plans for us. We have only begun to scratch the surface of what we can do with this town."

The group of men entered the small building they had gathered in front of and started to sit down at the tables throughout the room.

"Please, take a seat," directed the cloaked man.

"Thank you," replied one man and sat down.

"Joshua and his expedition have been derailed, so it is up to us to find that Midas Orb. If we do, we will be the richest men in the world. The powers of that orb are immeasurable."

"Immeasurable?" asked one of the men. "How can it be immeasurable?"

"You will know what I mean once you've seen it," continued the cloaked figure. He pulled the cloak down off of his head.

It was Segor!

"You all know what our plan is, right?" he asked them.

Calls of "Yes, sir!" resounded through the room, and every man nodded his head.

"Great!" Segor clapped his hands together and pulled out a map. "This is a map of the town, and I have already marked certain areas we will concentrate on. Of course, some we have already hit, but we must do more," he stated and pounded his fist onto the table. "Everybody here will be a slave to us before we will rest. Got it!"

"Yes, sir!" Again, a chorus of responses went up.

"Tonight has just begun for us. Let's get going."

Segor put the map away, walked out the door, and headed toward the center of town. The rest of the men dispersed and went their separate ways.

The night went by slowly for both Javan and Aran. Several times, Aran awoke, feeling someone watching him.

In a small building across town, the flickering light of a torch could be seen through a window. A figure moved about the shop, collecting things and putting them into a sack he carried over his shoulder. After pausing to close the sack, he threw it over his shoulder and left through a back entrance. The figure put out the torch and crept away into the night.

Javan, too, awoke one time with the feeling of being watched but let it go as just paranoia.

Through the window of the bank, several figures could be seen milling about the building. Suddenly, there was a small explosion, and the men ran into the back room. A light went on above the bank, and a man peered out the window. He turned and quickly threw on a nightshirt.

The men ran out the back of the bank building carrying several large sacks. One man tripped and spilled his sack all over the ground. Hundreds of pieces of paper fell out of the bag, and he sprawled on the ground trying to pick up as much as he could. The side door to the bank opened and a voice yelled, "Stop! The bank is being robbed! Stop them!"

The man on the ground got up, grabbed what he had in the sack, and fled through the woods behind the bank building.

"Help! The bank was just robbed," cried the man again, running into the center of the road.

Joshua lay on his back and tossed and turned all night long.

Lights started going on throughout the townsfolks' homes, and several men ran out into the road and headed towards the bank building. There stood a man in trousers and a nightshirt trying to pick up some of the pieces of paper left behind by the thieves. He placed them into a small sack he found in the bank. Someone came up to him as he put the last of the money into the sack.

"What happened? Are you okay?"

"Yes, I'm fine. They just robbed the bank," the man said, walking back into the bank. There he lit a torch.

Money was strewn all over, and there was a huge hole in the wall where the vault used to be. There were blackened pieces of rubble lying everywhere.

Lucas, sleeping on his stomach, also tossed and turned all night but never woke up.

Each man awoke in the morning, sore yet ready to conquer another day's adventures. They ate some of their breakfast rations and gathered up their gear. They decided to go through the twenty-foot-wide archway to the west.

"Is all of this really necessary?" asked Javan.

He noticed most everybody ached somewhere.

"Well, you agreed to go with me on this adventure," replied Joshua. "If you want to leave, be my guest."

"Nobody said that. We just wanted to know why we are really here."

"Let's just say that it will all be perfectly clear once we've finished our journey," responded Joshua.

"I hope so, but I am getting sick and tired of this," stated Aran, who put his breakfast rations away.

"I know," said Lucas. "So am I, but we really have to do this. Let's try and keep our spirits up."

As the men went through the archway, they entered what appeared to be a fountain room. The room had indigo-colored floor tiles with jade-colored tile surrounding the fountain and forming a ledge about two feet high. The men entered and looked around the room. In the center of the fountain was a statue of a grinning Imp. Not taking any chances, Javan drew his sword and cautiously advanced. When Javan reached a spot about five feet from the statue, the Imp animated and recited a riddle:

A narrow fellow in the grass
Occasionally rides
You may have met him—did you not,
His notice sudden is
The grass divides as with a comb
A spotted shaft is seen
And then it closes at your feet

And opens farther on
Several of nature's people
I know, and they know me;
I feel for them a transport
Of cordiality
But never met a fellow,
Attended or alone
Without a tighter breathing
And zero at the bone.
("The Snake" by Emily Dickinson)

Javan knew the answer to the riddle because of past poetry experiences, so he challenged the Imp. He didn't say the answer but drew his shield and stepped closer. The Imp abruptly and skillfully spit poison at him! Javan, ready, hid behind his shield to avoid being hit by the poison and then yelled out the answer.

"A snake!"

The Imp turned back into a stone statue.

Taken aback by Javan's knowledge of poetry, the rest congratulated him on a job well done. They found nothing of value in the fountain room, so the men moved on through the corridor in the center of the north wall. The corridor led to an armory.

The chamber was filled with all types of armor and weapons. There were two suits of leather, one suit of chainmail, and a suit of splintmail. There were ten quivers of arrows, a crossbow, a short bow, two long swords, and five daggers all strewn about the chamber. In a leather pouch, they found ten darts. Along the south wall was a morning star, a footman's flail, a throwing hammer, and a halberd, which was hanging from the wall. Further searching revealed a standing suit of splintmail. The suit held a long sword in its gloved hand. Almost daring something to happen, Javan reached out to grab the sword. As he did, the splintmail suit came to life and caught Javan in the side with a blow that threw him backwards several feet. With his side bleeding, Javan jumped up to his feet to attack. Joshua had already started the attack, and Javan jumped in to help. Javan was again hit by the suit of splintmail and knocked down again. Joshua missed but avoided being hit. That was just long enough for Javan to get up again. This time he was mad and swung wildly at the suit. Javan hit the suit dead center and completely sliced it in two. On his follow-through, however, he hit and knocked Joshua down. Joshua picked himself up and expressed his disapproval over being knocked down but nonetheless congratulated Javan on his fine job of killing the animated suit of splintmail.

"Sorry, Joshua," stated Javan as he helped Joshua up. "Let's look for a secret door. He must have been here for a reason."

"We'll each take a different part of the wall, and if you hear a hollow sound, that is probably it," explained Joshua.

Lucas and Joshua tapped on the west side while Aran and Javan searched along the east wall.

They tapped and tapped, not hearing anything that sounded different than a stone wall. After several more minutes still finding nothing, they decided to walk back into the fountain room past the Imp statue and back out into the huge ballroom. There they went through an opening in the northwest corner.

The opening they went through led to a corridor tiled in silver. At the end of the corridor was a door. Javan pushed the door open as he drew his sword. The door opened into someone's living quarters.

As they entered, the men could see the contents of the room: a huge gauze-curtain-surrounded bed in the center, a feminine-looking dressing table on one wall, and two large wardrobes on another. The men carefully entered the room and looked around for any sign of life. After a quick scan of the room revealed nothing as far as living things, they searched for anything else they could use. They found a large gold chest in one corner of the room.

Javan inspected the bed and found white fur strewn about it.

Joshua took a look at the gold chest and could see it was made of real gold! Drawing his shield for protection, he lifted the cover off of the chest. When nothing happened, he peered into the chest. He only saw soiled clothes, so he used his sword to take them one by one out of the chest. Then he tapped his sword on the bottom of the chest. He heard a hollow sound. He pushed on the bottom and quickly released it. It popped open to reveal another smaller gold chest. Joshua took that chest out and opened it. Inside was some jewelry: a ruby set in a gold brooch, a pair of emerald earrings in silver settings, and an emerald choker. Joshua tried to take out the choker, but it wouldn't move! Then he tried the earrings, but again they wouldn't budge! He grabbed the ruby and pulled the ruby out of the setting. In doing so, it revealed a small vial. He noticed the vial was empty, so he put the ruby back and walked over to Javan, who was still at the bed.

Aran found several pieces of silk lingerie inside the dressing table, most of which would be see-through if a woman were wearing them. He found satin see-through panties and satin see-through bras. He carefully searched through the lingerie but found nothing else of importance. He thought for a moment of what a woman would look like wearing the satin bra and panties. Suddenly, losing his concentration, he smelt the aroma of roses. He searched for the source of the aroma. At the back of a drawer he found a small pewter bowl containing fragrant dried rose petals. He also found a small vial of fragrant oil.

Lucas searched the wardrobes and found female clothes in one and men's clothes in the other. The men's clothes included several military uniforms. Lucas disregarded the clothes and found a drawer at the bottom of the wardrobe. It had a small pouch in it that contained juniper berries. He also found a small, locked wooden chest. With no thief around to pick the lock, he took his sword and banged it on the chest. The chest popped open, and out fell a gold orb. The orb was palm-sized and seemed to be solid gold! *Could this be the Midas Orb?* he thought. *Only one way to find out!* He grabbed his sword and scraped off a layer of gold paint. Underneath, the orb was a ball made of lead! Angrily, he threw the orb down to the floor.

Crash!

The sound it made when it hit the floor caused everyone, including Lucas, to turn around startled. They drew their weapons! The rest, not knowing what the ball on the ground was, learned of the real reason for their coming on this adventure.

"Okay, the real reason we are here..." started Lucas. "We have come here on this mission to find the Midas Orb. It has very special properties that are very unique to only the Midas Orb, but in the wrong hands and used for evil, it can cause death. So when I saw this gold ball..." Lucas picked up the gold orb from the ground. "I thought perhaps it could be the Midas Orb. The Midas Orb is made of pure, solid gold, so we should check every orb we see very carefully."

"What? You mean we are here on a scavenger hunt?" asked Javan.

"Well, kind of," replied Joshua.

"Great," replied Javan sarcastically.

"No, wait. Lucas and I came here to find the Midas Orb. No matter how long it took or how far into this castle it took us."

"I wish I had known of this before," stated Aran.

"Would it have made a difference in your coming along?"

"Maybe," said Aran. "I thought we were going to find treasure and take it home for our own good. Not some ball!"

"Do you always think of yourself, Aran?" asked Lucas. "Sometimes you have to think of others, too!"

"Right," sarcastically replied Aran.

"Hey, we can help out, right, Aran?" asked Javan with a pat on the back of his friend.

Javan gave Aran a hopeful glance that said nothing more than "maybe."

"What choice do we have now?"

"Probably none, but be careful," warned Joshua. "It has very, very strong powers. The Town of Gnarda would like to have it back in their possession, so they can live easier again."

"Why do they get the orb?" asked Javan.

"Because I said we would give it to them if we found it." Joshua explained, not revealing in the least the orb's real powers of turning any precious metal into gold upon touch. "It was stolen from them in a raid on the town, and I told them we would bring it back for them. There is a substantial reward for the return of the Midas Orb to Gnarda."

Javan knew that the Midas Orb was powerful and knew it had been stolen from the town, but he never thought he would get a chance to possess it. Only Javan and his partner knew that if they found it, they weren't going to give it back to the people of Gnarda. They would keep it for themselves!

The men explored the room vigorously, looking for the Midas Orb. After taking the tapestries off the walls, they searched by tapping with the backs of their swords on the walls. They listened for any sound of a hollow spot that would indicate a secret door.

After almost half an hour of searching and finding none, they decided it was useless and left the room.

They decided to take the passage to the west next. Javan was first, followed by Lucas, Joshua, and Aran. They walked down the corridor tiled in emerald green. When they got to the door at the end of the corridor, Javan drew his sword and pushed the door open.

Chapter 6

The town of Gnarda's sheriff's office had reports of four different incidents during the past night. One report at the general store included missing food sacks and tools. Another report was the robbery and bombing of the bank, including several thousands in monetary notes stolen and the bank considered a total loss. A third report was from an elderly couple living on the outskirts of town who had four pigs and two cows stolen. The fourth report was from a woman who reported her husband had been killed and herself raped by three hooded bandits who broke into their home. Missing in the robbery were several gold pieces of jewelry and her platinum brooch. She was at the infirmary for observation, and her husband was taken to the morgue.

Crime had gotten worse in the town, and the town leader didn't know what to do about it. He knew Joshua was off looking for the Midas Orb, but could he wait long enough for them to return—if they even returned at all?

Javan drew his sword and pushed the door open.

Roar!

There in front of the group stood a creature with a lion's body, huge wings of an eagle, and a human-like head. Javan, Aran, and Joshua turned and ran back down the corridor as fast as they could. They didn't even want to find out what that creature was or if he was guarding the Midas Orb! They called for Lucas when they reached the fountain room and waited for him to come. Lucas did not run. He noticed the creature as just a statue of an andro-sphinx with a magic mouth spell on it. He called back for the others, but there was no response. Several seconds later, he heard their calls and decided to go back to the fountain room to get them. He walked on, not believing a statue scared them. When he reached the fountain room, he found Javan, Joshua, and Aran standing in the far corner with their weapons drawn, ready for action. They had a puzzled look on their faces when they saw Lucas walk back into the room.

"Why didn't you run away?" asked Aran.

"Couldn't you guys see it was only a statue with a magic mouth spell on it?"

"What? No, I guess we couldn't," stated Javan. "I thought it was going to kill all of us in one mighty gulp. So I ran."

"Well, it was only a statue. Let's go back and see what it is guarding."

They glanced at each other, nodded, and headed back down the corridor.

They entered the room, and once again there was a loud roar!

This time, however, they knew what it was and were only slightly startled. As they entered the room and looked around, all they could see in the dark and musty chamber was a large wooden table. The table was in the center of the east wall. As Lucas walked past the table, he could have sworn he saw the table move. He stopped and looked back at it. Aran and Joshua rushed up beside him and told him that they also saw the table move. Javan, hearing of this, took some food out of his backpack and placed it upon the table. No sooner had he done this when the table quickly engulfed and devoured the food. Javan knew what it was and had experienced this type of creature before. Offering it more food, Javan asked the creature if it could tell them something they didn't know about the chamber.

"Hidden passage of secret there is," the creature said. "South corner. Leads to treasure."

"Thank you. Here," said Javan, offering the creature more food.

The men hurried to the southwest corner and started tapping on the wall with the backs of their swords. With one solid tap, Joshua heard a hollow sound.

"Hey! I heard a hollow sound! Right here," he exclaimed and tapped on the wall again.

The rest came over to him. Javan noticed the wall where Joshua was seemed a little bulged out. Javan put his hands on the wall and tried to push first to the left and then the right. When he slid it to the right, a section of the wall, not much bigger than a small door, slid into the other wall! He had opened it!

Before the men entered the corridor behind the door, Javan and Lucas lit new torches and tossed the dying ones aside. The corridor wound around for several yards and led them to another opening. As they came upon the opening, Javan and the others drew their swords, readying for action. They continued on.

The chamber they entered was made of all black tiles. As they entered the chamber, their torchlight seemed to disappear, making it very dark and hard to see. The walls seemed to absorb the light, so they could only see a few feet in front of them as they went on. They broke off in pairs, each with a torch, and worked their way around the outer edge of the chamber, searching along the walls for other doors or passageways. They found nothing and all gathered back where they had come in. Javan suggested they leave and not waste any more time.

Javan took a torch and led them through the door. He immediately disappeared, torchlight and all! Fearing the worst, the others ran through the door to find Javan.

Chapter 7

They stopped in their tracks and covered their eyes. The bright light almost blinded them! One instant, they were in total darkness, and the next, they were in total light.

After a couple seconds of gaining their eyesight, they turned to see where they were. They noticed they were in a chamber lit by three discs. Javan was there, too, holding a torch!

The chamber was about the same size as the one they had just came out of and made out of the same gray stone that most of the castle was made from. The discs were in the northwest and southeast corners. The men looked around further and could find no doors to the room. All they saw was a six-foot-tall obelisk, shaped like a three-sided pyramid. The obelisk was right in the center of the chamber. Along three of the walls were large wooden chests.

Slumped over in a corner next to one of the chests was a cloaked humanoid creature! Javan remembered seeing that cloak before and walked over and rolled the creature over. He could not believe his eyes! The entire group was astonished by who they saw!

It was Paleo!

He looked dead! His face looked a hundred years old, and his hands were withered and beaten. Not knowing if Paleo was dead or alive, Aran put a cure light wounds spell on him as Javan tried to revive him. A slight muffled moan came from within Paleo's body, and he fought for a breath of air. After some eyelid movement, he finally opened his eyes. When he saw the guys, he tried to smile. Joshua gave Paleo some rations and a drink of water. He took a cloth out of his shoulder sack, balled it up, and put it under Paleo's head for comfort. Paleo started to get stronger. His face regained some redness, and his hands regained some warmth. Paleo went from looking like a ghost one minute to at least a living person the next. Given the way they'd found him, that was a big improvement.

Javan told Aran to look after Paleo while he and the others checked out what was in the chests. Javan took the one on the north wall, and Joshua headed for the one on the east wall. Lucas found himself taking the last one, the one on the south wall.

Javan opened the chest with caution, but when he saw what was inside, he quickly flung the top open and grabbed the crown! The crown had a huge diamond in its center with gems radiating out from around it: four rubies, four emeralds, and two aquamarines. The crown was etched in platinum, and Javan estimated its value near ten thousand gold pieces!

Joshua opened up another chest and found a silver tiara inside. The tiara had a diamond center with radiating lines etched outward from it. He estimated the tiara's value at four thousand gold pieces!

Lucas opened the last chest and found over five hundred platinum pieces.

Bringing everything into the center of the room, Javan, Joshua, and Lucas had to find a way out of the room. With no doors and only a six-foot obelisk left to examine, they went up to the obelisk and started examining it. Seeing that it had a number in each corner of each side of its pyramidion top, they assumed that they had to do something with the numbers in order for the obelisk to do anything. The sides looked like this:

With his first thought to push the numbers in order, Joshua tried it, but nothing happened. Then, noticing that they were etched into the stone, he traced the numbers in order. Again nothing happened. Then they etched the numbers in the reverse order. Still nothing happened.

"I tried that much but had run out of things to eat and almost starved to death," said Paleo, who watched them struggle with the strange obelisk.

"Don't worry. We'll get out of here. You can count on that," stated Joshua. "There has to be a way."

"I don't have any ideas," stated Aran.

"Neither do I," replied Javan. "Just keep trying different things, I guess."

Both men went over and tried to help Paleo.

"Try something different. Do anything," complained Lucas. "Hurry."

With nothing working, Javan decided to try something different. With addends of seven on all three sides, he traced the seven on one side, the four, two and one on another side and the six and one on the last side. Still nothing happened. Lucas and the others had grown quite impatient. Their torches were going out, and the air was getting thick.

"Something has to work," complained Aran.

Javan threw a torch aside in disgust.

"We are never going to get out of here. I just know it," complained Javan.

"With that kind of attitude, you are right," said Joshua. "Let's try and keep a positive attitude. There has to be a way out, or there would be more bodies in here."

"Good point, Joshua," pointed out Lucas. "Let's try this."

They tried different addends of six—but still nothing. Paleo had recovered pretty well and crawled over to Lucas, who was next to the obelisk. Aran went over by Javan.

Paleo had watched everything they'd done so far and finally remarked, "Look for the same numbers on all sides."

"Why not? Nothing else has worked so far," said Joshua.

He noticed that only the number one was on each side, so Joshua traced all the numbers except the ones. He was distraught to find nothing happened.

"Try the ones," shouted Paleo a bit angrily.

"Doing it next," said Joshua.

Tracing the ones with his sword, Joshua remarked, "This has got to do it."

With those words, first one side and then the others started to open, top coming down towards the ground! They dropped outward to forty-five-degree angles and stopped. The obelisk was hollow inside!

The men noticed a circle etched on the floor inside the obelisk. They also noticed three sharply pointed daggers embedded in the interior of each side. They were placed about midway up the side. They appeared to be spaced so that they would meet when the sides were closed together.

"Let me try it out to see if we can get out of here this way," said Joshua. "I will step into the circle, and if the sides close on me, you guys try to stop them. If I am teleported out of here, I will try to get back in, so you know this is the way out of here."

"What if you get stabbed by the daggers in the sides of the walls?" quizzed Aran.

"That is a chance I will have to take. I don't know any other way out of here. Do you?" responded Joshua.

"No," they all replied.

"Well, then, somebody has to do something. So I will. If I don't return in an hour or so, keep trying to get out of here. You will know this way doesn't work." He stepped up to the first opening. "Here goes."

Everyone grabbed a side in case they started to shut on Joshua and waited. He carefully and slowly stepped into the obelisk and the circle inside. Suddenly the sides snapped inward and closed!

With the obelisk's quickness, each man was unable to keep a hold of his side, and it snapped shut in seconds.

Thinking quickly, Lucas etched the ones again. The sides came down again. There was no one inside! Joshua's footprints were on the ground but no Joshua!

"At least he didn't die," sighed Lucas with a slight chuckle in his voice.

"As far as we know," retorted Aran.

Just as Joshua stepped into the obelisk, it became pitch dark again. He heard the stone openings slam shut but did not get hit by the daggers. He didn't know where he was or if anything or anyone was near him, so he tried to feel ahead of him. He reached out with his hands and felt a solid structure. It was a wall—no, wait! It was a doorway! He carefully walked through it.

He took a couple of steps and grabbed a torch from his backpack. He lit it with his flint, and as the torch came to flame to light, Joshua realized he was in a room: the same room they had all just exited via teleportation!

He thought for a second, walked farther into the room, turned around, and walked back where he had come from. He vanished again!

The men waited anxiously for any sign of a living, breathing Joshua.

Suddenly, they heard a voice!

"Hello, guys," said Joshua with a big smile on his face.

All of them turned around, startled.

"What the hell!" shouted a startled Javan. He turned around to see Joshua standing there.

"Here I am, guys!" Joshua exclaimed. "I was transported out of this room and into the corridor right outside of the black-tiled room where we came from," he explained to the guys.

Joshua smiled and held out his arms for all to see that he was alright.

"Great! Now we know that is the way out of this crazy room," cheered Aran, who grabbed one of the chests and readied to leave.

One at a time, starting with Aran and ending with Javan, they all stepped into the circle and were teleported outside of the black-tiled room. Joshua's torch was still lit, so they moved on.

They walked back into the room with the strange table creature and the statue of the andro-sphinx. After another long day, they decided to sleep there for the night. They knew the table creature was friendly and that the magic mouth spell on the andro-sphinx statue would warn them of approaching danger, so they all lay down to get some much-needed sleep.

Chapter 8

Not long after the sun began to set, several cloaked figures moved about the town. They would slip in and out of the shadows and cross the roads in a flash of light. Elsewhere in town, a woman in an upstairs window pulled the shades and kissed her two children goodnight. In another home, an older lady placed a book upon a shelf, returned to her bed and turned out the light.

From the town stables there could be seen a small disturbance. The horses stirred and bucked as several men tried to herd them into the inner corral. One horse was being considerably stubborn and would not enter the paddock. Suddenly the horse kicked and bucked, throwing its stable hand to the side. The horse galloped off into the wilderness in a flash of speed. Several others ran over and jumped onto their horses and quickly rode off after the wild horse.

Across town, there was a woman peering out of a window. She turned around and drew the shade closed. She went over to the bed and sat upon it. She pulled her robe off and laid it neatly at the foot of the bed. When she got up and turned around to put out the light, she heard a noise from outside the bedroom door. She quickly pulled the robe back over herself and went to the door. Just as she got there, the door burst open, and two men in black cloaks came into the room. She went to scream, but one man covered her mouth and grabbed her. He threw her down onto the bed and sat upon her, holding her down so she could not move. The woman tried frantically to wiggle out of the hold the man had her in but to no avail. The second man searched through her personal belongings and filled his sack with several jewelry items and gold pieces he found in the room.

"What do we do with her?" one man asked.

"Fuck her, I don't care," replied the second as he kept on searching the room.

"I think I will," replied the first man. He pulled a rope from his shoulder sack and tied the woman's hands to the bed frame.

He then gagged her mouth and tied her feet to the foot of the bed frame. The woman tried desperately to get free, but the more she moved, the more the ropes cut into her arms and legs. She grimaced in pain. The man ripped her nightgown off of her and pulled down his pants. He got on top of her and proceeded to rape her. The woman fought frantically to stop him and get free, but she was tied down and couldn't get loose.

After the one man had his turn, the second man, who had finished ransacking the room, then took his turn with the woman. After the men took all they could, they dressed and left the woman to die. She was bleeding from her arms and legs and gasping for air. Her body was red and swollen from all of the abuse she had taken. She lay there waiting for someone to find her. Tears filled her eyes as she fell unconscious.

When the men awoke, they noticed the table creature was gone.

They gathered up their things and were off again. They walked back into the fountain room. Finding a new door on the south wall, they threw it some food and went back into the ballroom. The door proceeded to devour the food and retake its place as a door.

Joshua smiled as he saw this and glanced at the others.

With two archways not yet taken, the one on the north wall and the one on the east wall, they decided to go through the one on the north wall next. That archway lead to a hallway, and at the end was another doorway.

Meanwhile, Paleo had explained that he couldn't sleep the night that he'd disappeared, so he decided to take a torch and walk into the castle to see what he could find. The first archway he took was the one with the fountain room at the other end. Knowing the answer to the Imp's question, he passed without incident and proceeded on to the chamber with the andro-sphinx. Again, he wasn't fooled by the magic mouth spell and kept on going. He said the Mimic was not in the room the first time he entered. He found the secret passageway by accident and entered it, looking for treasure. He entered the dark room and tried to exit when he was teleported into the room with the obelisk. He couldn't get out and wished he hadn't left the group on his own—a little late, but he wished it anyway. He quickly ran out of rations and water. He could feel himself being drawn into a coma but could do nothing about it. He was all set to die when the others came to his rescue.

Javan pushed the door open, and they entered a huge ballroom-type chamber with a large table in the center. The table was constructed of highly polished oak. They were no chairs, but a gigantic chandelier had fallen from the ceiling onto the table at about its midpoint and shattered. Walking over to the shattered chandelier, Javan and the others could see quite a lot of gold pieces lying on the table and floor. Seeing the gold and getting greedy, each member started picking up gold pieces and shoving them into his shoulder sack.

They were so engrossed in picking up the gold that three stealthy boogerbears wandered into the room and initiated an attack!

The boogerbears rushed at them with their long swords drawn. Aran caught a glimpse of the attackers and took his chance to quickly chant a hold person spell. The spell went off just in time to trap two of the boogerbears and probably save Javan from certain death. Javan and Joshua drew their swords and attacked the third still-charging boogerbear. After a bloody battle, the boogerbear fell, but so did Joshua.

With Paleo hurting too much to help and Lucas busy killing the two trapped boogerbears, Javan and Aran saw their chance to split. They gathered up all the remaining gold pieces they could and any treasure the boogerbears had and headed through the doorway on the south wall. Lucas saw the two betraying their fellow party members and turned around and swung at Aran. Aran blocked the swing while Javan struck Lucas with his sword. Lucas was not expecting the attack and fell to the ground with a thud. He grabbed his side in agony.

"You have traveled far enough," laughed Javan as he and Aran walked on.

"I'll get you damn fools," yelled Lucas as he lay on the ground, trying to crawl towards Joshua to help him. "Someday I'll get you two idiots!"

Lucas had a tear in his eye as he looked back at Paleo and Joshua. Paleo was doing his best to bandage Joshua but was still too weak to turn the body over.

Lucas crawled over to Joshua and Paleo. All of them were badly beaten and needed rest desperately. They decided to stay where they were and rest there.

They dragged Joshua over to the wall and propped him up against it, and there they rested.

Javan and Aran went through the chandelier room and into what looked like a kitchen. There were several utensils hanging from the ceiling and large butcher-block tables around the room. Javan and Aran, fearing Joshua and Lucas were right behind them, didn't stop to search the room but instead went on through the room into what appeared to be a barracks chamber. There was no one in the chamber, so they searched, quickly, through the beds, finding several platinum pieces. They left the barracks through the door on the north wall and entered a gray stone corridor with a very-well-worn path trod down the middle. They also saw deep scratches or gouges running the length of the corridor that led to a set of double doors.

"It sure looks like something pretty damn heavy has been dragged through this hall and through those doors," pointed out Javan.

"Let's see where these doors lead," replied Aran.

He walked over to the double doors and pushed them open.

The doors opened into stables. The gouging in the floor continued across the stables to a set of doors on the east wall. There was light coming from behind the doors. Javan walked over to the doors and slowly pushed one open.

"It leads outside!" he exclaimed after peering behind it.

"Cool, but we can't leave until we have that orb in our possession," reminded Aran.

"Right, but now we have another way out of this castle in case we need it."

Javan and Aran shut the door and walked back into the castle. They examined the floor and ceiling and went into one of the stalls to see what they could find.

"Holy shit!" yelled Javan as he stopped in his tracks and turned to run. "Run!"

"I can't! I'm caught," stated Aran in distress.

They were caught! They could not move and could see a giant spider heading towards them!

"Fuck! What do we do?" screamed Aran as he looked around for a way out of the mess.

"Quick! Use a spell! I'll use magic missile," Javan replied.

"I don't have any that would work right now, Javan! Get the hell out of here!"

Javan's magic missile spell went off and hit the giant spider right in the head. The giant spider reeled from the blow but took one mighty leap and was upon them!

Javan and Aran were stuck in the spider's web and could only attack with their one free hand, so that was exactly what they did!

Aran held the giant spider away from Javan with his swinging sword while Javan prepared another magic missile spell.

The spell went off! In a bright flash of light, the giant spider was burned to a crisp! After several seconds, the blast of smoke from the burning spider had cleared, and they could see that the giant spider was dead.

Javan and Aran used their swords to cut their way free. They were shaken and exhausted from the thought of being eaten by a giant spider. They turned around to leave the stall when suddenly they saw another gory sight! Another giant spider was right in front of them, its mouth opening and closing as if it could already taste its prey!

Aran had nowhere to go. He was trapped. He could see the spider's venomous fangs coming right towards him! He screamed for help! Javan got his burning hands spell ready and attacked the giant spider with his sword.

As Javan's spell went off, the giant spider bit Aran!

"Aaaaah!" screamed Aran, who felt the venom from the giant spider rush through his body.

Aran was pumped full of deadly venom and screamed as loud as he could from the pain. He had only seconds to live and knew it! Javan was terrified at Aran's screaming and wildly swung his sword, hitting the spider several times. The giant spider dropped to the ground in a pool of blood, but Aran fell with him.

Javan could see the giant spider's fangs clinched around Aran's waist and could see his expressionless face. He knew it was too late for his partner. Aran was dead, poisoned by a giant spider! Javan, nauseous and weary from the sight of Aran's dead body, slumped over and threw up before falling to the ground and passing out.

Chapter 9

One woman locked the door and flipped the open sign to closed. Another turned the safe lock and put away the last of the day's gold receipts. They both headed back behind the counter to count the remaining jewelry pieces. Suddenly, several men burst into the goldsmith's shop and grabbed the two women working behind the counter. The women tried screaming but were quickly gagged and their hands tied behind them. One man broke open the safe and filled his sack with the gold pieces inside. Another took one of the women into the back room and tied her to a wall fixture. There he ripped her blouse and skirt off her. She stood there with only her bra and panties on, trying to get free.

"Not bad, not bad at all," stated the man, reaching out to fondle her breasts.

The woman struggled to get free, but the ropes just cut deeper into her arms every time she moved. The man ripped her bra off...

In the other room, another man grabbed the other woman and brought her into another room of the shop. There he tied her to the desk and ripped her blouse off her. He broke the clasp on her bra and threw it to the floor. He roughly grabbed her breasts and squeezed them in his hands. The woman frantically tried to get free but couldn't. The man ran his fingers down her sides and grabbed her skirt. He pulled it off of her and grabbed her panties. Quickly he ripped them from her and fondled her again.

The third man continued putting into his sack anything of value. Then he joined the man in the back room of the shop. As he walked into the room, he noticed a whip hanging on one of the walls in the supply closet. He grabbed it and brought it with him into the room. The man had the woman against the wall raping her. She cried and struggled to get free but couldn't. When the man finished raping the woman, the other one came up to her and held out the whip.

"Want to feel real pain?" he asked.

She winced and tears rolled down her eyes. She shook her head.

"What? I couldn't hear you. Would you like to feel real pain?"

She shook her head again. She had a frightened look upon her face, and tears continued to stream down her face.

The woman stood before the two men completely naked. The second man poked at her breast. She winced in pain.

"Come on, that can't hurt. I barely touched you," he said and put both hands over her breasts and began to squeeze them harder.

"Feels good, huh?"

"Yeah, she did. Real good," responded the first man, who had finished pulling his pants back up and was now holding the whip.

"Well, that's too bad they don't listen better when we ask them something, huh?"

"Yup, too bad." The first man slapped the whip on the ground.

The woman winced in pain at the sound of the whip.

"Oh, look, she is afraid of the whip. Why don't we show her what real pain is?"

"Okay, you first, Nahor."

"Oh, thank you, Jacob."

Nahor grabbed the whip and started to whip the woman. Welts quickly formed across her chest, and she cried in pain.

Smack! Again he hit her. She groaned in pain every time the whip hit her, but there was nothing she could do. Her chest started to bleed from the whipping, and her stomach was red and swollen.

Smack!

This time, the whip caught her legs, and they burned with pain. She screamed in agony!

In the other room, the man had the woman up on the desk and was on top of her raping her. He heard the whip sounds and got off of her.

"That gives me an idea," he said as the woman looked on with fright in her eyes.

He went over to the corner and picked up the lantern. He brought it closer to the woman, who winced in pain the closer he brought it to her.

"Let's see how hot it can get before you can't take it anymore, okay?"

She shook her head in fear.

"Speaking of hot, you are hot! I must say, I could have done worse. Well, I suppose I could give you a break this time, but just remember who your master is, okay?"

She nodded her head in agreement.

He put the lantern down and buckled his pants back up.

"Don't worry. I want you around for future considerations," he said and turned and walked out of the room.

He got to the back door just as the other two men came by. They all left through the door and left the woman tied up and bleeding. The first woman, on the desk, finally freed herself and ran into the other room to help her friend. She gasped as she reached the room.

Her friend was propped against the wall and had blood coming from her chest, stomach, and legs. She was barely breathing. The woman untied her friend and helped her get some clothes on and then carried her out of the shop to get some help.

"We'll get whoever did this and make them pay for it," she told her friend as they crossed the road for help.

Lucas, Paleo, and Joshua awoke refreshed and ready to go. After some breakfast rations, they went through the door that Javan and Aran had taken hours before.

The corridor was made of plain grayish-brown stone. The stone walls were smooth and flat just like most of the others.

They continued down the corridor for several hundred feet and came upon a door. Lucas took to the front and cautiously pushed the door open as the others drew their weapons ready for action. Lucas peered in and didn't notice any moving objects, so he proceeded into the room.

The room appeared to be a kitchen. There was a fire pit in the one corner, several large chopping-block tables at various places throughout the room, clay pots, pans, and utensils hanging from the ceiling over the tables. Cautiously but quickly, they examined the pots, pans, and utensils. They also examined the chopping-block tables. They found nothing.

Next, Lucas walked over to the fire pit. Seeing ashes in it, he reached in and felt for any heat. He couldn't feel any. Paleo, who was standing next to him, looked in and noticed the flue was closed. He reached in and opened it. Just as he pushed it open, five large bat like creatures, or as he knew them Strigas, dove down and into the room! They swiftly flew around the room and circled back and attacked Paleo. They all grabbed swords and shields and tried to attack the Strigas.

Several Strigas rapidly bit Paleo. He fell to the ground as he was not quite back to one hundred percent following his last attack. He cowered on the ground and tried to cover up and avoid their attacks. With two Strigas on him and sucking his blood, Paleo cried for help. Lucas and Joshua killed two of the Strigas and then ran forward and tried to get to Paleo.

Paleo could feel the blood being drained from him, but there was nothing he could do. He flailed around trying to get them off of him. Lucas attacked first and quickly killed one of the Strigas that was attached to Paleo. Paleo slowed in his attempts to get the Strigas off of him. Suddenly his arms went limp, and he stopped fighting! Horror struck Lucas and Joshua as they killed a second Striga. Just as they did, the final Striga bit Paleo and began sucking his blood!

Joshua grabbed the Striga in his hands and pulled it off of Paleo. He brought it over his head and threw it as hard as he could against the ground. The Striga bounced from the impact and skidded across the ground. Joshua stomped on it in a murderous rage.

The sound of cracking bones and squishing flesh was followed by a mess of blood and bones on the ground.

Lucas quickly applied bandages to Paleo's wounds, but there was no way to return the lost blood, and he feared Paleo had lost too much.

"How can we stop him from dying, Joshua?" asked Lucas with a tear in his eye.

"I have no idea, pal! I have no idea! I can tell you one thing, though."

"What's that?" asked Lucas.

"These damn Strigas won't bother us anymore."

"But Paleo is going to die!"

Lucas looked for anything to help Paleo, but there was nothing!

Joshua walked over to the fireplace and said, "I better close that flue again."

He reached up and slammed the flue shut!

With nothing else to do, Lucas and Joshua laid Paleo down on one of the tables. They stood by his side in case he needed anything. They didn't know what to do to help him or if there was anything they even could do! Paleo tried to speak but was too weak for words. He even tried to smile but couldn't. He was helpless!

"Don't talk, Paleo, buddy," directed Lucas. "Just save your strength."

Lucas could feel that Paleo was barely breathing, and it seemed to be getting worse. He checked his eyes and could tell Paleo would not make it any further. Lucas began to cry for his friend.

"There has to be something we can do for him!"

"I'm afraid not, Lucas," consoled Joshua. "He has been too badly beaten and lost too much blood."

"I won't accept that! I won't!" screamed Lucas.

Lucas searched around for something, anything to help their friend. There was nothing around that might help.

Both men knew it was the end of the line for their friend, so they knelt down and prayed for him. Paleo was as white as a ghost again and lay motionless, never again moving. Both men had tears streaming down their cheeks as they watched Paleo take his last breath. With a slight jerk, Paleo's hand fell loosely by his side, and his body fully relaxed. Both Joshua and Lucas felt as though a part of them had just died, and for a long time they didn't even move an eyelash. They couldn't believe what had happened so quickly to their friend. Both men wept for Paleo and arose and picked him up. They wanted to put him in some safe place where no Orcs or Goblins would find him and feast on him. They took him back to the room with the broken chandelier and then into the chamber with the continual light discs. There they tried to exit by way of the door. It was still locked, so they placed Paleo's body, covered, into one of the alcoves behind the gold curtains. They left all of his possessions with him and said one last goodbye to their friend.

"Goodbye, pal. I'm gonna miss you," wept Lucas.

"Come on, Lucas, we'd better get going again. There is nothing we can do now. It was Javan and Aran's damn fault."

Joshua reflected with a menacing growl on his face on how they had been betrayed and abandoned in their time of need.

"Don't ever say those two names again!" shouted Lucas, who turned away from Paleo and wiped his eyes clear of tears.

"I'm sorry. Come on."

Joshua took Lucas by his arm and led him away from Paleo's burial vault.

They walked slowly back into the ballroom and then into the chandelier room. The two didn't really feel like continuing, but they told the officials in town they would find the Midas Orb, and that was what they were going to do. They walked back into the kitchen, noted the spot where Paleo was killed, and then went on through the doorway on the west wall. The corridor was made of stone. The corridor led into some sort of pantry or closet. The small room contained several barrels and bags of foodstuffs. Lucas searched through the food, finding it untouched and in good condition. The barrels and bags contained wheat flour, rice, pickled cucumbers, cauliflower, carrots, and dried, salted fish.

Tasting some of the fish, Lucas said, "Maybe we should take some of this stuff. It tastes pretty good, and we are running low on supplies?"

"Yeah, maybe we should. It does look pretty good," replied Joshua, who reached down and grabbed some of the dried fish.

He ate some.

"Try some of these cucumbers, Joshua. They really taste great!"

Lucas handed Joshua some pickled cucumbers and grabbed one for him.

"Mmmm, mmmm."

They ate some and put some of the rations into a sack, which they tied to their backpacks.

While they were doing this, Lucas noticed some flour and shredded sacks on the floor seemed to move. With his sword, he poked into the shredded mess. Suddenly there was a screech, and eight giant rats came scampering out. Lucas and Joshua quickly ran for the door. They just made it in time to squish one of the rats in the closed door!

"Should we fight them? They might have gems in their nest," Lucas asked.

"Let's fight them, but we'll wait and fight them in the pantry."

"Good idea. We can't lose to rats!"

So they waited about five minutes until they were sure that the giant rats had returned to their nest. Joshua pushed open the door and rushed in. He didn't see any movement, so they both moved over to the nest of shredded sacks and slammed their swords into them. Lucas felt his sword hit something, so he withdrew it and kicked the nest. From within came four giant rats and three babies.

Joshua and Lucas really had no trouble killing the giant rats. They sliced most of them in two like they were made of paper, and the rest scampered away or were stepped on. There was a puddle of blood and guts when they were through. Joshua used his sword to drag the nest out into the open.

He saw two more dead rats, which he must have killed when he drove his sword into the nest the first time. He dug around in the nest and found several gems: two clear gems (rock crystals, fifty gold pieces each), two clear, pale blue-green gems (zircons, fifty gold pieces each) and one golden-yellow gem (topaz, fifty gold pieces). There was nothing else, so they decided to leave the pantry and go on. They went back into the corridor outside and took it to the north.

The corridor was made from nondescript gray stone. It ended with a door that opened into another chamber. This chamber appeared to be barracks containing several cots and a band of eight Orcs. The Orcs were busy looting the cots and overturning everything in the chamber when the group walked in. Lucas and Joshua readied for a fierce fight, one which they hoped would not be their last.

They quickly ran to the nearest Orc and slayed him before the others even knew what had happened. The slain Orc slumped to the ground at their feet without even mumbling a word. Standing side by side, Lucas and Joshua readied for more. One by one the Orcs came at them, and one by one they fell. In a matter of minutes, only three were left. Those three surrounded Lucas and Joshua and attacked simultaneously so that during every strike, one would be able to hit its mark. The first time, Lucas was hit and almost lost his balance. He would have fallen into Joshua and sent both of them to the ground, but he retained his composure in time to fend off another blow. Only a second later, Joshua was hit by one of the Orcs. He fell to his knees and tried hard to defend himself. He had his shield up in front of him and his sword out swinging at anything near him. Lucas killed an Orc and had badly beaten a second when Joshua was hit again. This time he fell face down on the ground. Lucas jumped over him and warded off any more blows from hitting him. Lucas then killed a second and third Orc before they could hit Joshua again.

Lucas didn't feel like losing another friend, so he quickly bandaged Joshua, stopping the bleeding almost immediately. Lucas knew Joshua would be okay for a while, so he searched the Orc bodies and found eight platinum pieces on each. He put them into his shoulder sack and returned to where Joshua was. Joshua had sat up and regained some of his strength when Lucas got back to him. He slowly got to his feet.

While Joshua continued to recover from his injuries, Lucas took the time to explore the contents of the chamber. He found several overturned cots with bedding scattered about. The whole barracks was generally disturbed. He also found several swords and items of armor: two chainmail suits and one platemail suit along with a long sword and a short sword. Sensing the short sword as magical, he strapped it to his backpack and continued searching. He lifted up a sheet and found a ring underneath it. The ring was gold! Joshua had walked over to where Lucas was and tried to help. Lucas decided Joshua should wear the ring in case it was a ring of protection. Joshua put the ring on, and it fit. They continued to search but found nothing else in the room, so they decided to leave.

Chapter 10

Javan woke up and found himself lying next to a dead Aran! *I must have blacked out*, he thought, feeling very sick. Everything that had happened lately was too much for him to handle. He gagged and threw up. He wiped his mouth and regained his composure. He decided he had to continue. He had to. He was on his own now and had to find *that* Midas Orb.

Javan walked through the door to his left. There were two large anvils and several different tools hanging from the walls in this chamber. Javan figured it used to be a blacksmith's chamber. Still shaken, Javan decided to move on. He walked through a door in the west wall and entered what looked like an outside garden area.

The garden had no ceiling and was arid and desolate. As he peered around the area, he noticed a well in the northwest corner. The well had a pail and about thirty feet of rope tied to it, resting on its edge. Javan also saw a section of the area where there were vines and overgrown bushes. He was exploring the underbrush and thought he saw something move! Just as he made a move to grab his sword, he was caught off guard by a giant scorpion. He froze, hoping the giant scorpion would forget him and move on. That was a mistake! With one quick jolt, the scorpion caught Javan in his pinchers and lashed out and stung him in the back with his venomous stinger!

When the stinger hit him, it hurt like hell, and Javan winced in pain. He tried to get free. He could not pry himself loose from the scorpion's pinchers and started to feel the venom surge through his body. It moved from his back towards his heart!

Within seconds, Javan found it hard to breathe. He gasped for air but could get none. His arms and legs started to go stiff. He tried to move them but lost control of them. His struggles got less and less aggressive as the poison took over his body.

The scorpion turned around and carried its victim back into its lair. The scorpion put Javan down, and Javan took his last breath. He was dead!

Lucas and Joshua walked through the door into a small corridor. The corridor was made of gray stone, and there was a well-worn path, lighter in color than the surrounding area, down the center. There were deep scratches running the length of the corridor leading to a set of double doors at its end.

"Something very heavy must have been dragged through here. Look at how deep those gouges are," stated Lucas and pointed to the ground.

"Right you are, but what could it have been?"

Lucas and Joshua followed the gouges through the doors into stables. The gouges continued across the ground to another set of doors on the east wall.

"There is light coming from behind those doors," said Joshua.

"Maybe it leads outside," said Lucas, who was excited about the thought of fresh air and sunlight.

"Hey, what say we find out?" said Joshua as he walked over to the doors.

He pushed one open. There was a bright light that came through the door. Both men put their hands over their eyes to shield them from the bright light. Several seconds later, they were able to see out the door through the light. It was the outside of the castle. They both stepped into the door frame and took deep breaths of fresh air.

"Ah, it sure feels good to get some fresh air for a change," stated Lucas, who took another deep breath and sat down.

"It sure does. It sure does, buddy," stated Joshua, who also sat down for a bit.

"I wonder where exactly this part of the castle is in comparison to the front entrance?" asked Lucas, looking around and at the countryside.

"Well, the sun is to our right by about thirty degrees, so I would guess this is directly north of the front entrance. Maybe it is a bit east, but it looks like it should be directly north of the entrance we came in," responded Joshua.

"You're pretty good at this kind of stuff, aren't you?"

"I have had teachings in charting and mapping using the sun and its directions, but most of it was a guess," replied Joshua and chuckled.

"Ha, ha, ha. That's what I thought."

"Had you going for a bit though, right?"

"Yeah, right. Joshua?"

"Give me a break. It would have worked on the women," stated Joshua.

"But I am not a woman, am I?" asked Lucas.

"No, you are not, and thank goodness for that," stated Joshua. He got up and patted Lucas on the back as he turned and went back into the castle.

"Now we know another way out," stated Lucas, "in case we need a quick exit." He got up and followed Joshua back into the castle.

"Yes, but we have to find that orb, Lucas!"

"Right, let's go," said Lucas.

Joshua pulled the doors shut, and they continued on. They had only taken a few steps when they were stunned by what they saw only a few feet ahead of them. They thought they were going to be sick. Not more than ten feet ahead of them was a giant spider!

They quickly drew their swords and looked for a way out, a way to avoid the giant spider.

"Looks like we might need that exit, Joshua," yelled Lucas.

"Wait," he said in response.

He noticed the spider had not yet moved.

He took a step closer to it. He squinted his eyes as he looked at the spider and noticed that the spider was actually slumped to the ground. They both cautiously moved closer step by step, ready in case the spider came to life. They looked closer at it and could see two huge burn marks on the side of its body.

"Looks like he's already dead," stated Lucas.

"Sure does," remarked Joshua, poking at it with his sword to make sure.

The giant spider did not move.

"Whew! That could have been a tough one," sighed Lucas as he put his sword back into its scabbard.

They carefully walked around to the head of the giant spider and noticed a human figure on the ground. Taking extreme caution, they moved closer to the figure. They could see the spider's mouth parts dug into the side of the victim and knew he had died from the spider's poison. The figure looked strangely familiar to them from the back, but they couldn't tell who it was for sure. With one end of a sword, Joshua pushed the body over so the face could be seen. They gasped at the sight!

It was Aran!

His face was as white as a ghost, but they could still tell who he was. He still held his magical mace in his hand and had dried blood covering his body. Both Lucas and Joshua hated Aran and Javan for deserting them, but they knew that this was a very horrible way for anyone to die!

Well, with Aran dead, they figured that Javan had either left the castle or had also died. They didn't figure he would continue on by himself, but then again, crazier things had happened so far on this journey.

Joshua spat on the body of Aran and cursed his spirit.

"Hey, do you really think that was necessary, Joshua? He is already dead. Have some respect for the dead, man," scolded Lucas.

Joshua turned to look at Lucas and had a scowl on his face.

"I don't care if he is dead. I hate that son of a bitch more and more every minute I see his body," screamed Joshua, who kicked the body in disgust.

"Save your energy, Joshua. You'll need it. Let's check out the giant spider's lair. That orb could be anywhere."

They searched the closest stall and found six platinum pieces. Four of the stalls had nothing more than hay and dung in them. When they got to the sixth and final stall, they saw another horrid sight. Another giant spider!

After a brief adrenaline rush and a chaotic rush for their swords, they realized this one was also dead. Its body was badly burned and beaten. Several of its legs were dismembered from the rest of the spider's body. As they peered into its lair, they could see several platinum pieces strewn about. Lucas quickly grabbed what he could, and they left the stall.

They hurried to the next chamber through the door on the west wall. Two dead giant spiders and Aran's dead body were more than enough for them to have to deal with for one day. They walked through the door and into what appeared to be a blacksmith's chamber.

The chamber had two large anvils in it along with several different tools hanging from the ceiling and walls. Almost knowing there was nothing in the chamber they quickly gave it the once over and left through a door on the west wall. They entered an outside garden.

The garden had no ceiling over it and looked very arid and barren. Lucas noticed a well and overgrown vines and brush in the northwest corner of the garden.

Joshua was immediately drawn to the well. His curiosity drove him ahead. He saw a pail with a rope tied to the handle, so he picked it up and lowered it down into the well. It went down about twenty-five feet before he heard it hit water. As it hit the water, five large spiders came scurrying out of the well and ran towards Lucas! Joshua, letting go of the rope, quickly drew his sword and attacked the large spiders. Lucas also drew his sword and took three steps backwards to avoid getting all five spiders on him at once. Both men swung their swords at the large spiders. The large spiders never got close enough to attack either Lucas or Joshua as they killed them with ease.

Realizing that when he let go of the rope, the pail fell into the well, rope and all, Joshua searched for a way to get it back out. There wasn't any that he could see. Lucas turned around and decided to check out the overgrown brush and vines. They got within twenty feet of the brush when Lucas noticed a spot of dried blood on the ground. He also noticed that the grass was matted down in a trail leading into the underbrush. Lucas told Joshua about it, and they quickly drew their weapons. Lucas peered into the brush and could see a giant scorpion! It was alive! Lucas saw that the scorpion was busy eating something. The scorpion was tearing pieces of flesh away with its pinchers and devouring them.

Lucas was so engrossed in trying to see exactly what the scorpion was eating that he didn't notice that the scorpion had stopped eating and was moving towards him. Lucas was busy staring at a bloody head and a bloody suit of black platemail lying on the ground.

The scorpion was only a couple of yards away when Joshua noticed that it had moved towards them.

"Lucas, run!" he yelled and turned, grabbing Lucas's arm as he did so.

Both men quickly ran back into the castle. As they ran, they looked back over their shoulders to see how far ahead of the scorpion they were. Only about twenty feet separated them from the scorpion! They ran through the entrance to the chamber and into the corridor straight ahead of them. There they waited, with weapons drawn, for the scorpion to enter.

Several minutes had gone by, and there was no scorpion, so Joshua grabbed his bow and arrows and readied them, aiming them at the door they had come through earlier.

"I'll go in and try to kill it with arrows. I am anxious to see what's in his lair," Joshua said as he started to move back to the garden.

"Ah, I'm not so sure about that Joshua," replied Lucas grabbing his arm.

"Lucas, we have to. As soon as I see it, I'll shoot the arrows, and with any kind of luck at all, I'll kill it without it even knowing what hit it." Joshua moved forward, and Lucas released his grip on his arm.

With Lucas just a few feet behind him, Joshua inched into the garden. He could see the scorpion heading back towards its lair. Joshua told Lucas to get ready to run, and he drew an arrow and fired. The arrow missed! It fell several feet short. He quickly drew another and fired again, this time with more force.

Lucas yelled, trying to get the scorpion's attention. The scorpion turned around and darted towards them just as Joshua let the arrow go. The arrow sailed straight and true and hit its mark. The arrow was lodged in the scorpion's head! The scorpion writhed in agony. Joshua had just enough time for one more shot, so he drew and fired again. Another direct hit! Lucas turned and ran back into the castle while Joshua waited a bit longer to see what the scorpion would do. The scorpion didn't move. It hadn't seemed to die but had two arrows stuck in its head and had just stopped in its tracks.

Lucas, on a signal from Joshua, came forward and saw the strange thing that had just happened. Of course, they weren't going to go out there and fight the scorpion hand to hand because it may be playing a trick on them, but they had to find out if it was dead or not.

"Be careful, Joshua. He may not be dead yet!"

"I know," replied Joshua, who drew another arrow into his bow. "Creep along the wall, and see if it follows you. But be very careful, and don't get too close to it."

"Okay, are you ready?" asked Lucas.

"Yes. Go ahead," replied Joshua and pulled the bow up to his eye to get ready to fire.

Lucas stepped into the garden and inched his way along the wall, trying to draw the scorpion away from Joshua, who was ready to fire again. As he did, Joshua noticed the scorpion's eyes follow Lucas and the tail jerk up and head towards him!

Joshua, with the skill of an avid archer, adjusted his angle and fired at the scorpion's tail. The arrow hit the tail and ruptured the poison sac. The arrow shot right through the tail but had hit its mark! Blood and poison, a light yellow in color, oozed from the wound. Again the scorpion writhed in agony.

Lucas was a bit startled by the scorpion's quick actions but continued inching along the wall. He was only ten feet away from Joshua and moved toward the center of the garden away from the wall. The scorpion's eyes continued to follow him, and Joshua drew another arrow. He was putting it in his bow when the scorpion lunged for Lucas. He caught him in one of his pinchers. Joshua fired an arrow but this time missed the target!

He dropped the bow, drew his sword, and rushed towards the scorpion. He heard Lucas scream!

The scorpion brought his tail over his head and quickly stung his victim! Lucas screamed when he was stung. Joshua hoped there was no poison left and that it had all oozed out when he ruptured the tail with the arrow.

Joshua attacked the pincher that held Lucas. Lucas was pounding on the pincher and screaming in pain! The hold kept getting tighter and tighter. With four chops to the pincher, Joshua completely chopped it off and Lucas fell to the ground. The pincher released its grip, and Lucas got to his feet to help Joshua fight the scorpion. The scorpion veered around toward Joshua but missed guarding any attack by Lucas, so Lucas saw his chance and attacked. He was a bit stunned by the damage the scorpion had done to him, but he mustered enough strength to hit the scorpion's head twice with all his might before the scorpion slumped to the ground and died.

"That scorpion will never again give us any trouble," yelled Joshua as he and Lucas made sure the scorpion was dead, both striking it several more times.

Pausing for a moment to catch their breaths, Joshua and Lucas walked over to the vines and brush where the scorpion had its lair. They cut through the vines and brush and entered its lair. Inside were the dismembered parts of two or three creatures, the newest of which was Javan!

"Oh my gosh," said Lucas and turned away, coughing.

"Wow! What a way to go!"

"Pretty bad way to go, wouldn't you say?"

"Yes, but he had it coming," said Joshua, remembering what had happened earlier in their journey.

They reluctantly searched the scorpion's lair and found Javan's magical sword, a large shield under which was a horde of three thousand silver pieces, three thousand gold pieces, and six gems, each worth about one thousand gold pieces. Everything else in the lair was worthless, only torn pieces of armor and weapons that had been destroyed by the years of weather. Lucas felt sick from the sight and suggested that they leave as soon as possible. Joshua agreed.

Chapter 11

"What is being done to stop the crime in this town?" asked one of the townsfolk.

"When do we get relief from all this? Women are being raped and people murdered!" stated another.

"Yeah, and several others have been kidnapped," stated another.

"And I've been robbed twice already in one week!" shouted another.

"I'm afraid to go outside anymore!" yelled one woman.

"Please, people. We are fully aware of the situation at hand," stated the leader of the town. "We are doing what we can. I suggest that you just give in to these barbarians, and in due time, they will get caught."

"Give in to them? Are you crazy?" yelled one man. "I'll kill them if they come by my home!"

"In due time—what the hell does that mean?" asked an elderly man.

"Yeah, what does that mean?" asked another. "And I agree. I am not giving in to anyone. What's mine is mine, not theirs!"

"People, calm down," said the town leader. "Everybody gets caught sooner or later," he continued. "We have caught several of them in the past day. Please bear with us. We have people working it."

"Bear with you? Our lives are at stake here, sir. With all due respect, I don't have to bear with anyone," sarcastically stated one man.

"Please," pleaded the leader, "we are doing all we can. There just isn't enough help for us. There are too many of them for us to handle right now."

"What can we do?" asked one man.

"Yes, what can we do to help?" asked another.

"I suggest you don't get involved. Just keep your homes locked, and always be aware of your surroundings when you go outside at night," cautioned the leader. "We just have to use common sense and be careful of who we talk to and where we go. It will all be taken care of shortly, I promise."

After some mumbling amongst themselves, the townsfolk started to disperse and head home.

"I hope we can hold out long enough," whispered the leader to his assistant.

"I hope so, too, sir," agreed the assistant.

Both men walked back into the chamber room and took off their meeting garb to go home to their families.

"Joshua, I'll go this way," said Lucas, pointing ahead of him. "You go that way." He pointed to the west. "Stay within shouting distance of each other, and return here in about five minutes."

"Gotcha," replied Joshua, who turned around and walked to the west.

Both men walked about twenty feet before Joshua shouted, "I've found stairs leading down. I'm going to go down them and find out where they lead. Then I'll return, okay?"

"All right, but be careful, Joshua!" Lucas shouted back in agreement.

Lucas went another twenty feet before he entered a chamber. He couldn't see anything, so he decided to return to their meeting place and tell Joshua what he found. Reaching their meeting spot, he could see Joshua rounding the corner and coming toward him.

"The stairs led to a chamber which appeared to be a wine cellar, but I saw three black objects roaming around inside, so I quickly left," reported Joshua.

"I found a chamber," said Lucas. "Maybe we should check out the chamber I found first?"

"We'd better. I have no idea what is down in that cellar."

"The chamber didn't have any doors in it, so we can't go any further than that anyway."

"Good. Lead the way, Lucas."

They walked to the chamber. Both men entered. The chamber was rather oddly shaped and had a cot in the northwest corner, and there was a wooden chest in another corner. Along the west wall of the room was a large desk strewn with sheets of parchment. There were diagrams and unfamiliar scribbles on most of the parchments.

Joshua, more interested in the chest by the cot, walked over to it while Lucas continued his search of the desk.

Lucas found a letter cylinder lying on the desk. He untied the two leather straps and lifted the cover off the cylinder. He noticed a sheet of parchment rolled up inside, pulled it out, and unrolled it. It was a scroll with a dispel magic spell on it. Lucas knew neither he nor Joshua could use it, but he decided to put it back into the leather cylinder and take it anyway. Also on the desk was a brass key on a leather strap. Lucas put the cylinder and key into his shoulder sack and went over to Joshua.

Joshua had walked over to the chest and checked to see if it was locked. He pulled up on the handle, and it opened easily. He found only dirty clothes inside. There were several pairs of pants as well as a black and green shirt. There were also a couple of other pieces of clothes in it, but he did not examine them any further. The cot had clean linens and a pillow on it. Joshua checked under the cot and under the mattress. He found nothing. He saw Lucas coming toward him, so he rejoined him by the south wall.

Along the south wall of the room was a shelf upon which rested twelve corked containers. Lucas reached up and took one down. The vial had a small symbol on it that looked like this: ∝. Neither one knew what the symbol meant. Even after Lucas gently shook the bottle, they couldn't tell what might be inside so they opened it.

The vial had a clear red liquid in it. Joshua, the more daring of the two, decided to taste a little bit of it. First he smelt it. It didn't have any odor to it. When he touched the liquid to his mouth, he felt a cool sensation but only took a small sip.

"There is no taste to it. Nothing has happened... Awww!" cried Joshua. He fell to the floor and grabbed his stomach.

Lucas dropped down to his knees beside Joshua, not sure of what to do to relieve his pain. Joshua was still breathing, and his eyes were open. Lucas could tell he was in pain although he didn't know what had happened to Joshua. Lucas gave him some water to drink from his canteen.

"Are you all right? What happened," he asked.

"I guess so. I don't know what happened. It just felt like a small explosion inside my stomach," explained Joshua as he rubbed his stomach. "Good thing I only took a small portion, or that may have been my last drink."

"Wow! You really scared me, Joshua. I thought you were dying," sighed Lucas.

He wiped the sweat from his brow.

"No, I'll be all right in a minute or two." Joshua sat down on the ground.

"Okay, but let's not taste the contents of any other vial. Okay?"

"I can't disagree there, pal," said Joshua, who slowly got back to his feet.

Joshua reached for another vial and opened it. When he did so, there was a horrible odor that came forth. It smelt, to Joshua, like animal sweat. Perhaps that was what it was, but Joshua didn't care. He closed the vial and returned it to the shelf. He took down another vial and opened that one up. The vial contained feathers from a Hippogriff, nothing of importance to Lucas or Joshua, so they corked it back up and put it back on the shelf. They took down another one and opened it.

Inside was a thick, red liquid. It looked like blood, but neither of them was sure of what it was, and they weren't going to try to taste any of it after what happened the last time they tried that. They put the vial back and took another one. This vial had a symbol on it that looked like this: ?. Inside the vial was a greenish, milky liquid. The liquid didn't have an odor, but Joshua still suggested they not try any of it. The next vial also had a symbol on it: ᏉᎧ. The vial had a blue, milky liquid in it. Joshua could remember taking a blue liquid on an earlier adventure, but he couldn't remember what happened to him. He just remembered waking up in the hospital and feeling very sick.

"I don't think we should take this one either," said Joshua.

"I don't think we should take *any*," repeated Lucas. "This is most definitely a very weird collection."

"It sure is. Let's just see what's in the other vials before we go on."

"Okay," answered Lucas, who put the last vial back on the shelf.

The next vial had a symbol on it that looked like this: ☦. Inside was a pinkish liquid.

"Let's take this one," retorted Joshua. "I know what kind of pinkish liquids there are, and all of them that I know of are good for you. In fact, most are a type of healing potion."

"How do you know this one is good for you? It might be made to trick someone like you or me."

"True, but I'm going to take it anyway," said Joshua.

He then drank a huge gulp and waited.

"See! Nothing bad. In fact, I feel refreshed, not sick. Take some!" Joshua handed the vial to Lucas.

Lucas took the vial but hesitated just a moment longer. He wanted to make sure nothing happened to Joshua before he took any of it himself.

"Well, as long as you haven't winced in pain yet, I guess I can take some." Lucas took a big gulp of the pinkish liquid.

"Hey, this stuff tastes pretty sweet, and you're right; it does make you feel refreshed."

"Yes," agreed Joshua. "Let's take a look at the others now."

"Right, but be careful though. Just because one is good for us doesn't mean any others are."

"I know, but let's see what else is in here."

They both reached up and grabbed vials. Lucas opened his first. Inside was a huge white pearl!

"Wow! I figure it at five hundred gold pieces. What do you think, Joshua?" asked Lucas, showing Joshua the pearl.

"You're right about that one, but look at this vial. It has a symbol on it, and contains a clear liquid in it. That's probably not a good sign."

"Probably not as most poisons are clear. Put it back," said Lucas, putting the pearl in his shoulder sack.

He reached up for another vial, this one full of milky, gray liquid. The vial had a symbol on it: ❄. Lucas decided not to take any chances and returned the vial to the shelf.

Joshua took down another container and opened it. Inside were hundreds of very thin fibers.

"They look like hair of some sort but are very, very fine," reported Joshua.

He put it back and took down the last vial. Lucas started to search other parts of the room while Joshua opened up the vial.

The vial was full of insect legs. Disgusted with the strange collection of items, he rejoined Lucas by the door.

"It doesn't look like much in here," said Lucas, "or we probably would have found it by now."

"Right, but it could be behind a secret door," stated Joshua as he pounded on parts of the walls, listening for any hollow sounds.

"If it is, it can stay there as far as I'm concerned," replied Lucas.

"I agree, but the Midas Orb isn't gonna be sitting out in the open. It's gonna be hidden, so I think we need to do what we can to try and find it."

"Okay," Lucas sighed. "I'll help you search."

He wished they could leave the room as it gave him the creeps, but he knew they had to find the Midas Orb, or the whole journey would have been for naught.

They spent several minutes examining every part of each wall in the chamber but found nothing. They decided to leave and headed back into the other chamber and then went down the steps to the wine cellar.

As they entered the wine cellar, several large cat-like beasts with large tentacles coming from their shoulders surprised them and attacked.

The odds were against Joshua and Lucas from the beginning, but both men were skilled fighters and quickly evened the fight. The beasts surrounded the two men and attacked in rounds, flailing their suction-cupped tentacles at them. Joshua and Lucas missed being hit quite a few times before Joshua got bit in the leg by one of the beasts.

Joshua, bad leg and all, killed one and then badly wounded another before Lucas could even get in a blow to the beasts. Joshua took two more blows from the beasts large tentacles before he killed it. Then he ran over to Lucas's aid and helped him battle the last beast. The beast had blood covering its entire body when it finally fell to the ground and died. Lucas and Joshua looked at each other and sighed. Suddenly Joshua was hit from behind! One of the beasts he knocked down wasn't dead and had gotten back up and attacked him! The beast was all over his back before Lucas had a chance to react. Joshua lay on the ground helpless while Lucas swung his sword at the beast. After several solid hits, he finally killed the beast and pushed the dead body to the side. Joshua sat up, groggy, but he seemed alright. He sat a while to recover some strength and then got up ready to go on. Lucas bandaged his back with some pieces of cloth and stopped the bleeding.

Three of the walls in the wine cellar had racks with bottles of wine on them. There were probably more than five hundred bottles of wine in total in the wine cellar. They searched the racks, pulling out bottles of wine and looking for secret doors. When they got to the middle section on the second wall, Lucas noticed that several bottles didn't come out of the rack. Instead, the bottles in that rack rotated in a clockwise, counter-clockwise circular motion. Lucas alerted Joshua to these different bottles and started turning them in a clockwise direction. When all that would turn were turned, he stepped back. Nothing happened! Lucas and Joshua decided to turn them in the other direction, counter-clockwise. As Lucas turned the final bottle, a part of the wine rack moved, and a secret door opened up behind it. The secret door opened into a corridor. After twenty feet or so, the corridor split into two more corridors.

Joshua and Lucas walked on with their swords drawn and their shields up. They went down the corridor to their right first. They came upon another corridor that went both to the left and right. They went to the left until they came to another door. Joshua pushed the door open and peered inside.

The chamber was lavishly furnished in gold and white. There were several plush, comfortable sofas, three furs on the floor, and two globular oil lamps. Joshua was the first to notice two statues of women, one in the northeast corner and one in the southwest corner.

Joshua, cautious of anything coming alive, walked up to one of the statues to examine it. It looked to be of pure gold and as far as he could tell was a perfect replica of a beautiful young girl. The statue was about five feet high, and the girl in the statue seemed to have a terrified look upon her face. She was dressed in a lacy nightgown. He tried to imagine what she would look like if she were a real woman.

"Hmmm," he commented.

"What?" Lucas asked.

"Oh, nothing. I was just wondering what this woman would look like in real life."

"Pretty great, probably," replied Lucas as he headed towards the other statue. "I'll check out the other statue."

"Yeah, I bet you will," joked Joshua, who looked around for anything else of importance.

Lucas reached the second statue and examined it. He noticed that this statue was also of pure gold and also a perfect replica of a very beautiful young girl. Again it stood about five feet tall, but the girl in this statue was undressed and was looking back over her shoulder like she was trying to avoid something or someone. She had a nightgown draped over one arm but appeared to have been naked at the time of the statue's formation.

Both men noticed nothing else unusual about the statues and knew that they would not be able to lift or carry them, so they decided to search for the Midas Orb elsewhere in the room. Joshua walked over to the sofas and started searching there. Lucas examined the furs and lamps, searching for any clue to the whereabouts of the Midas Orb.

Suddenly Joshua yelled, "Help!"

"What the hell is wrong?" responded Lucas, spinning around.

He could see a giant snake had coiled himself around Joshua's waist and stomach and was in the process of applying pressure to him, trying to suffocate him. Lucas ran over to Joshua and took out his dagger, trying to cut the snake in two. The snake quickly uncoiled and started slithering away. Lucas threw his dagger at the snake with one hand and drew his sword in the other. He hit the snake with his dagger and cut part of the snake's body before it crawled to safety under one of the sofas. The snake left a trail of blood but got away.

They decided to leave the chamber but not by one of the doors on the east or west walls; instead, they went back to the last fork in the corridor and headed to the right. There they took the corridor until they came upon a door on the right. They took that into another chamber.

The chamber they entered had a black, oily substance covering the floor. Joshua and Lucas investigated it further to find out it was some sort of crude oil.

"It is oil," stated Lucas. "We better be careful not to light it on fire, or it may end up taking us with…"

As the words came out of his mouth, he noticed something in the center of the chamber and stopped talking.

"What is that in the center of the chamber?" He pointed to something in the center of the chamber.

"I have no idea," replied Joshua. "Let's take a look at it."

Lucas followed Joshua into the chamber, taking every step with grave caution as to not slip on any oil. When they came upon the object, they noticed it was a trap door. The door in the floor didn't have any handle.

"It doesn't have a handle on it," commented Joshua. "Wait. Let me try to pry it up with my sword."

"Good idea, but be careful," cautioned Lucas, who backed up, so Joshua could get at the door.

"Here goes," said Joshua as he used the sword as a pry bar.

Joshua tried to lift the trap door with his sword, but it wouldn't budge. Joshua tried harder and harder when suddenly something gave way. Joshua jerked the sword up into the air, hoping he had done it. The sword tip and a piece of wood went flying into the air! Joshua saw this and was disgusted.

"Damn it!" cursed Joshua. "That was my magical sword!"

"Now it has lost its magic," replied Lucas sarcastically.

"I know that, Lucas. Damn! Maybe I can still use it as a sword though, huh? Do you think so?" Joshua kicked at the door.

"I hope so. For our sakes, I hope so," replied Lucas, who patted Joshua on the back giving him reassurance that he still stuck by him, no matter what.

They turned to leave the chamber and decided to go back into the chamber with the statues of the girls and rest there for the night.

First, they wanted to make sure the snake was dead. They searched under the sofas and found its dead, coiled-up body under one of them. Joshua used the damaged sword to pick the snake up and drag it into another chamber. They then made a spot to sleep and lay down and easily fell asleep. *It has been a long day*, remembered Joshua silently as he lay on the floor resting. Aran and Javan had turned up dead, and several new adventures had tested their fighting abilities. *What will tomorrow bring for us?* he wondered as he drifted off to dreamland.

Chapter 12

Back in town...
From the shadows in the back room came a figure. It moved towards a man behind the counter. With a quick, skilled gesture, the figure struck the man in the head and knocked him out. The man slumped to the ground, bleeding from his head. The figure quickly emptied the cash box and headed for the back door. From outside came two men carrying supplies for the store. The figure dashed into a closet and waited for a chance to leave without notice.

The two men dropped the cartons in the back room and went towards the front room. As the first passed the closet, he stopped for a moment. He thought he heard something! The figure inside the closet decided it was now or never. He burst out of the closet and struck the man with his shoulder as he went past him. The man fell to the ground and cried aloud as he did so. The second deliveryman was behind the first and saw what had happened. He drew his dagger and plunged it into the figure from the closet. He felt it cut through the leather armor and into skin. The figure screamed in pain and hit the ground, grabbing his side. The first deliveryman got up and pounced on the figure holding his arms down along his sides. The figure tried to kick his way out of the hold, but the second man grabbed his feet and held him tight. Both men shouted for help.

"Help us! We have caught one of the robbers! Help!" they both screamed.

From the front storeroom came the man that had been hit over the head. He carried a sword and poked it at the man on the ground. His head was still bleeding, but he stood very assure of himself.

"Ha, you picked the wrong man to rob tonight!" he screamed as help came from the back doorway.

Two other men came running into the backroom and helped hold the intruder down. They quickly tied his feet and hands and pulled him upright.

"What do you have to say for yourself now?" asked the storeowner, the man who was hit over the head in the front room.

The figure shrugged his shoulders and sighed in disappointment.

The two extra helpers carried the would-be thief outside to a waiting horse wagon. They threw him into the wagon and rode off to the town jail.

Joshua woke up in the arms of a very beautiful young woman. She was the most beautiful girl he could ever remember seeing. She was gently caressing his cheeks with her soft, silky hands. He was startled at first, but she calmed him. Gently she spoke to him about how she had found him there all alone and decided to sit with him through the night. She remarked at how handsome she thought he was and kind of turned away, embarrassed, when she said so. Joshua was bewildered about what she said about his being there alone and looked around. She was right! No Lucas! He was scared but then realized that he and the girl were alone in the room. He felt worried about Lucas but for some reason didn't feel like trying to find him. He felt a strange calmness while she touched him. He decided that with such a beautiful girl in his arms, why fight it? All his worries were calmed, and he relaxed again.

He reached up and gently caressed her cheeks as she had done to him. He suddenly realized he was on a bed and dressed in a new pair of pants and a clean shirt. He noticed that this young woman who was holding and caressing him was dressed in a white lace nightgown. The gown opened down the front and had slim cloth straps holding it closed. The V-neck collar came down just far enough to reveal the beginnings of the smooth curves of her breasts. Joshua felt himself forget about the real, dangerous situation he was in and reached up and kissed the girl. She let him kiss her and then got up from the bed. Joshua was confused at first but then relaxed again when he saw what the girl did.

She stood at the bedside facing him and started to untie the straps that held her nightgown on her shoulders. Then she turned around and bent over to take off her slippers. When she bent over, Joshua could see her bare ass. She did not have any underwear on! Joshua could feel the blood rush through him, so he took off his shirt and pants and lay in the bed, waiting for her. He couldn't help but stare at her ass all the while she stayed bent over. She stood upright again with a big smile on her face and turned towards Joshua. She slid the night gown down the rest of her body. Joshua could not wait any longer. This voluptuous woman was making him crazy! He reached up and pulled the girl into the bed. Joshua kissed her again. He pulled her closer and kissed her breasts. Her body was totally his, and his mind raced at the thought of what he could do with her. They lay there making love for what seemed like hours until suddenly the girl stopped Joshua and got up and out of the bed.

Joshua, puzzled by her suddenly stopping him, watched her put her nightgown back on. She had given him a good workout, but why did she suddenly stop? He was definitely puzzled. The girl put on her slippers, kissed him on the cheek, waved goodbye, and then walked right through a wall and disappeared!

"What in the world?"

Joshua rubbed his eyes and checked the walls. No girl! What had happened? Had it all been a dream? Where could she have gone?

"No way, it couldn't have been a dream. It couldn't have been! It seemed so real," he said as he flopped back onto the bed. He closed his eyes, trying to figure out what had just happened.

He was confused, but sleep came back to him, and he dozed off shortly thereafter.

Lucas was just coming to when he felt something on his forehead! He tried to jerk up but was restrained. He opened his eyes to see a very beautiful young woman holding him in her arms. He was lying on a bed, and she was next to him with only a white lace nightgown on. The V-neck collar came down just enough to reveal the beginnings of the rounded curves or her breasts. Lucas was startled. Where was he? Who was this very beautiful woman lying next to him? Why was she here with him. and why didn't he seem to care?

The girl spoke and answered all of his questions. Lucas gasped! He'd never asked the girl those questions; he just thought them, yet she answered them as if he had asked her out loud. Something was not right! Lucas finally noticed that he and the girl were the only two people in the room. Where was Joshua? The girl relaxed him again and caressed his cheeks with soft, silky hands. She said that she thought he was a very attractive man and that she hadn't had a man for a long time. She blushed after having said this. Lucas knew what he wanted to do, but somehow she held him poised in the position he was in. He had no willpower to resist the girl! For some reason, he didn't even want to fight the girl. He wanted to stay where he was and love her.

She got out of the bed and stood there facing him. She started untying the straps that held her nightgown to her shoulder when she suddenly stopped and bent over! He gasped! She didn't have any underwear on ,and her bare ass was right there in front of him! He fell into a frenzy of passion and lust. *What a perfect ass she has!* he thought. He wanted her—and badly! He stared at her ass, and when she stood up, she turned around again. Now she faced him and could see him sweating. She smiled, untied the straps holding her nightgown together, and let the nightgown fall from her body. The gown fell off her breasts, down past her waist and legs to the floor. She was completely naked standing there right in front of him! He started with her face and let his eyes examine her whole body. When his stare reached her feet, he reached out and grabbed her. He was led on by lust. He pulled her towards him. She fell softly to the bed onto her back. Lucas kissed her. He was going crazy! He wanted her now!

She was the most voluptuous woman he had ever seen, and he wasn't going to let this situation pass him by. He kissed her again, letting his hands caress the girl.

This fine young woman had given her body to him, and mad, crazy thoughts of what he could do to her raced through his mind. They lay there for what seemed like hours, making love and gently caressing each other. Suddenly she stopped him and got up and out of the bed. *Why? What have I done wrong?* thought Lucas. He reached for her, but she stopped him again.

She put on her nightgown and again bent over to put on her slippers. Lucas again reached for her, but she turned around and smiled. She kissed him on the cheek, waved goodbye and then walked right through a wall and disappeared! Who was this girl who'd come into his life and then just vanished? Lucas got up from the bed and searched for a secret door that she may have gone through. There was none—at least none he could find. What had just happened to him? Had this all been a dream?

No, it was too real, he thought.

Lucas was still sweating and breathing heavily from the lovemaking.

"It couldn't have been a dream. It just couldn't have been! It was too real! Look at me. I'm exhausted from it all. It had to be real."

He fell onto the bed wondering what had happened and slowly fell back to sleep.

It just couldn't have been a dream was his last thought before falling asleep again.

Joshua was the first one up, and he saw Lucas lying near him. He sighed and lay there waiting for him to stir. He rubbed his eyes.

"Perhaps it was a dream. No, it couldn't have been. Man, it seemed so real though," he said to himself as he thought about the night's experience.

Several minutes later, Lucas awoke and also sighed when he saw Joshua. "Wow! What a dream!" he exclaimed as he, too, rubbed his eyes.

Both men got up feeling very refreshed and ready to go. Each looked around as if he was lost and then realized they were in the same chamber they went to sleep in last night. The sofas and everything else was all still right there where it had been when they went to sleep. Each man proceeded to explain the dream they had the night before and realized they both had the same dream. Even the girl was the same in both!

"Wow!" exclaimed Joshua. "What a dream! I hope I have a real-life encounter like that one last night."

"Me, too! It sure seemed to help us relax though. I don't think I have had that good a rest since we started this journey. Look how refreshed we feel today. Ready to go!" explained Lucas as he noticed the major improvement in their dispositions.

"Right! Well…what do you say we get going while we still feel so good?" said Joshua, who got up, gathered up his belongings, and started to move on.

"I'm right behind you, buddy," Lucas said, also picking up his belongings.

They tried to open the trap door in the chamber with the oil in it again, but again, it did not open for them, so they left it alone and proceeded to another chamber.

They went farther north and came to some steps leading down into a chamber. The chamber had a pool of water covering the entire northern section of it. Bubbles were coming from the north side of the pool. They walked as far to the edge as they could and looked into the water. They could see the water was flowing and flowed underneath some steps leading into the pool. They looked around the chamber and could see a number of small urns lining one of the walls. Upon a closer inspection of the urns, Joshua saw they were made of clay and not of any real value. There was a door in the southeast corner, so they decided to take the corridor that lay beyond it.

They walked into another corridor. Joshua noticed the only features of the corridor were the two small holes near the floor on the south wall. Lucas peered through one of the holes but couldn't see anything. It was dark on the other side. He took out a small piece of wood not any larger than a pencil and lit it on fire from the torch. He pushed it through one of the holes. It landed hard on a hard surface and did not go out. It stayed lit. Lucas again peered through the hole and could see what appeared to be a bath tub made of tile. There were steps leading up into it but not much else. Lucas peered through another hole and discovered the same thing there too.

"There must be some way of getting into that room," said Lucas, "but I don't see any here."

"Maybe it comes off of another chamber," suggested Joshua, looking around for the answer. "Like the chamber where we slept last night. Remember, there was another door in that chamber, but we chose not to take it."

"You are right, Joshua! Let's go," said Lucas, getting up to leave.

"I'm right behind you!"

Both men walked back into the poolroom and then into the chamber where they spent the night before. They saw the statues of the women and were reminded of last night's experiences.

They took the door in the south corner of the chamber. They walked through the door and found a corridor made of a very highly polished stone. They came to two doors in the east wall of the corridor. Joshua pushed open the first door. Inside was a feminine-looking bedroom which two more cat-like beasts had taken over as their lair! Joshua quickly shut the door, and they went to the next door. Joshua cautiously opened it, remembering what was behind the last door.

The chamber was another feminine-looking bedroom. Joshua could see a wardrobe, a double bed, a nightstand, and several other things usually found in a woman's bedroom. Suddenly he spotted a young woman sitting on the bed! Both men recognized her as the one from their dreams. They looked at each other. At first they had puzzled looks on their faces, but then they both smiled. Maybe it wasn't a dream after all! They entered the room as the girl watched them. She didn't seem too surprised to see them but sat still and said nothing.

"Do you speak common?" asked Lucas.

"Yes, I do! What would you two like?" she replied, standing from the bed and revealing a short white nightgown. "I was just getting up from my rest."

Both men looked at her and then at each other and smiled again.

"What I would like," started Joshua, thinking about last night, "is for you to lie down on the bed again, and then I'll come over there and show you..."

"Stop that, Joshua!" Lucas said, cutting him off. He slapped Joshua on the shoulder. Of course, he also would have preferred she lay out on the bed for him, but he kept his cool and decided to stop Joshua before he said something he would regret later.

"Well, you have to admit, Lucas, she is a very attractive young girl—ah, pardon, young *woman*," Joshua said to Lucas while staring at the girl.

"Maybe, but we can't take advantage of that," said Lucas extending, some sort of respect for the half-naked girl in front of them.

"Wait, guys," responded the girl. "Nobody takes advantage of me unless I want them to! Okay?" She stood with her hands on her waist.

"Yes, sure," they answered in unison.

Joshua and Lucas walked over to the girl and asked her why she was there by herself.

"I was one of the general's harem girls," she explained. "The other girls were turned into gold when they didn't satisfy the general, but I hid from him and avoided his wrath."

"You mean, you didn't satisfy him either?" asked Joshua looking at her and not believing that could have been.

"Meaning," she responded, "I didn't want to." She sat back on the bed and rested on a pillow, crossing her legs.

"How long have you been here?"

"Not sure," stated the girl.

She showed no signs of being annoyed by their questioning and just sat on the bed answering any questions they had for her. Both Joshua and Lucas also seemed more relaxed and rested upon their swords by the edge of the bed.

"One question... Do you know where the Midas Orb is?" Lucas thought he might catch her off guard.

"The what? Nope, never heard of it. Don't even know what you are talking about," she replied. Suddenly she sat up and continued, "But I'll tell you this; if you two are looking for it, then I'll help. The only thing I ask is that you help me get out of here. I'll tell you more about my story as we go."

She stood up from the bed and walked over to the dressing table. She noticed Joshua's eyes had not left her since he walked into the chamber.

"I don't know if we can allow you to come with us. This is a pretty dangerous place," stated Lucas.

"Yes, it does get pretty scary at times," interjected Joshua.

The girl ignored their statements and continued on to the dressing table.

"I've heard screams and shrieks of a man being tortured at all times of the day, but I haven't found where those screams are coming from," continued the girl.

Standing with her back to the men, she let the nightgown fall from her body.

The girl stood naked in front of them, and all they could do was stare.

Her body was perfect! She had a perfectly bronzed, perfectly shaped ass. When she leaned over to get her blouse, they could see the outline of her left breast. She glanced over her shoulder to see if they were still watching her and didn't seem to mind that they both *still were.* She went on to put on a light blue blouse.

"Maybe it is the general himself, for I believe he is still alive," she said as she pulled on a pair of khaki-colored pants.

Joshua turned to whisper something to Lucas when they saw the girl pull up her pants.

"That *is* the girl from my dreams last night," he whispered to Lucas. "I'd know that body anywhere!"

"I know," replied Lucas, trying not to be heard by the girl. Lucas, unlike Joshua, decided right then and there that he was going to find the Midas Orb before sex this time.

She turned around to face them as she finished buttoning up her pants.

"I also know the general's wizard, Wthai, if I remember the name correctly, has been gone for a long time," finished the woman as she stepped into her knee-high leather boots. "Alright, let's go!"

"Do you have any weapons?" asked Joshua, trying to see if she needed any protection.

"Nope, I just use my hands. They are the deadliest weapons I know. Let's go, men," she said as she waved and walked past them towards the doorway.

"Okay," responded Lucas. He let her walk past him into the corridor outside.

"By the way, what is your name?" asked Joshua, glancing at her as she walked by. Her blouse fit loosely over her chest.

"Oh, my name..." repeated the woman, who noticed Joshua staring at her and gently touched him on his arm. "Just call me...Venus!" She smiled.

"Okay, Venus. Let's go," repeated Lucas, who tried to get the two going.

They walked out of the bed chamber and went north until they reached another door.

"What is behind the door, Venus?" Lucas asked.

"That is the bathing chamber."

Joshua pushed the door open, and they cautiously entered.

They saw a white-tiled bathing chamber with two blue-tiled bathtubs in the northwest and northeast corners. The bathtubs were approximately thirty feet by twenty feet in size with rounded corners facing the center of the chamber. Each tub had four steps leading down into it. There was no water in either. He walked over to the one in the east corner and was ready to peer in when a giant spider scampered out of the tub!

Venus screamed and ran for the door. Joshua and Lucas followed with the giant spider right behind them! The giant spider made a lunge for Lucas, and although it missed nabbing him full on, it did manage to trip him up. Lucas sprawled headlong into the door! Joshua turned around and swung his sword at the giant spider, inflicting a wound to the giant spider's head. The giant spider retreated several steps and waited. Lucas struggled to get up with Venus's help when the spider attacked again! This time he caught Venus with a hairy mandible!

Joshua pulled Lucas to his feet and attacked the giant spider. He first hit the spider's two front legs and then his head. He hit the giant spider with such a force that the spider let go of Venus and quickly dragged itself back to the east tub. The giant spider half-stumbled, half-climbed back into the tub. Joshua turned and grabbed Venus and Lucas and took them into the corridor. Then he slammed the door shut.

"Are you two alright?" he asked after making sure the door was secure.

Venus grabbed Joshua and held him tight. He held her back.

"Thank you for saving my life," she said, pulling him even closer.

Lucas and Venus were shaken up but not hurt, so they rested for a bit to regain their composure and strength, and then they continued on.

Chapter 13

They went down the corridor to the lounge room and entered the chamber. Inside they saw four human men.

Before Joshua or Lucas could even think, Venus sprang forward and slid feet first into two of the men, knocking them down. They didn't even know what had happened. Venus got back up and ran towards another. As she neared him, she crouched down and just missed being hit by the man's long sword as he turned around. She didn't hit him but stood back and waited for him to make his next move.

Venus was a human female. Her only weapons were her hands and feet and an occasional dagger she might find.

Meanwhile, Joshua and Lucas fought the three other men. They were outnumbered by one but managed to even the score. The first man fell with a deep gash to his chest and a nice, long cut to his right arm. Joshua got hit in the leg by the second man's sword but connected with a driving blow that leveled the man with a deep, bleeding gash to his chest and several other cuts to his back and arms. While the third man was fighting for his life, Venus was waiting for the fourth man to make a move. He finally advanced, and Venus was ready! She jumped into the air and kicked at the man's arm with the sword. He pulled away the sword and grabbed her foot. Venus landed hard on the ground and didn't move! She had been knocked unconscious! The fighter quickly pulled out a loop of rope and tied her hands and feet together. He then gagged her.

The third fighter was making it hard on Lucas and Joshua, so neither saw the fourth fighter drag Venus through a doorway and into another chamber. He placed her on a circular bed in the center of the boudoir, tied her to the bed post, and then went to a side shelf and grabbed an ebony coffer. He held the coffer over his head and waited by the doorway in case someone entered the boudoir.

Through the entryway came the third fighter with Joshua and Lucas right behind him. When Joshua and Lucas entered the boudoir, the fourth fighter hit Lucas over the head with the coffer. Pieces of the coffer went everywhere, and some strange gas poured out from the broken coffer. Lucas went down with a thud! Joshua could see Venus tied up and on the bed, but the gas was making him lose control of his muscles. He, too, went down with a thud!

When Joshua and Lucas finally came to, they found themselves tied up. They had no armor or weapons. When Joshua scanned the room, he saw Venus tied down in the center of a bed. She didn't move! Most of her clothes were torn, and she had blood running down her arms. She had red slashes on her sides and legs. It looked like she had been whipped! Her blouse was torn and bloody; her pants were soiled and torn; and her leather boots were at the foot of the bed. He did not see anyone else around.

Joshua frantically tried to untie his hands, but the harder he tried, the more the restraints cut into him. He finally gave up.

By now, Lucas had come to and was also trying to free himself from the ropes but with no luck.

"Venus!" yelled Joshua. "Venus!

"Hey," warned Lucas. "If she is sleeping, let her sleep. If she is dead, yelling won't help."

"Damn it, Lucas! What the fuck happened?" He looked around for anything he could use to free himself.

"When I get out of here, I am gonna track those two down and fucking kill them with my bare hands," he stated. He struggled again with the ropes around his hands and feet. "They better not have killed her!"

"You against those two?" asked Lucas. "My money is on you, Joshua."

He smiled at Joshua and also tried to get free from his binds.

"You okay?" he asked Joshua.

"Yeah, just fucking sick of this shit," he replied and yanked his arms again.

He looked up at Venus again. "Venus!" he shouted again.

"You really fell for her, didn't you?" said Lucas, who noticed the way he looked at her helpless body just lying there.

"Yeah, I guess so. I think she's perfect! Did you see that body?"

"Yes, I did, brother. Yes, I did. She has some pretty good stuff," replied Lucas again, tugging on his bound hands.

Both men made a quick jerky glance at the door when they heard it creak open. The two fighters came back into the boudoir carrying a chest of coins and two long swords. Both men were talking amongst themselves when they entered the room, and upon seeing Joshua and Lucas, they started to laugh. One walked over to Venus and shook her.

"Wake up! It's time for some more fun. This time while your men are watching! Wake up," demanded the man, shaking her again. Her head flung back and forth, but she did not move!

Then he looked at Joshua and said, "Too bad she didn't cooperate a little better though she did give us a lot of fun." He smiled.

"What do you mean?" asked Joshua.

"Well," the man paused. "We wouldn't have had to pump her full of sedatives if she had cooperated more and not been so active."

"Damn you! When I get out of here—" started Joshua. He struggled again with the ropes.

"When?" asked the man. "No, you mean *if* you get out of here."

The man laughed and walked over to the other fighter as Joshua tried to spit on him. He turned to slug Joshua but held back as the other fighter called to him.

"Leave him alone, and get over here!"

"You're lucky," shouted the man to Joshua.

"Sure, I am! You're the one who is *lucky*! You're lucky I am tied up right now."

Lucas sat by and watched all of it but paid more attention to the two men talking and what they said.

"When are we going to leave, Japeth?" asked one man.

"As soon as the girl wakes up and we can get our stuff together," the man, obviously Japeth, responded.

"What will we do with those two?" asked the other man, pointing over to Joshua and Lucas.

"Seth, don't be ignorant! We leave them here, but we make sure they can't get out."

"Right," he said with a giggle in his voice. 'When is Segor getting back?"

"Soon. Now go sit down, and don't ask any more stupid questions," demanded Japeth, obviously irritated by Seth's constant questioning.

Lucas, upon hearing that Segor was involved, almost blew up. Lucas remembered what Segor had done to them back at the dung-eater's cell, but he kept all remarks to himself for now. Suddenly, Venus started to stir!

Seth went over and lay down on the bed next to Venus and watched her as she started to wake up. Upon seeing him lying next to her, she struggled to get free, but Seth just pushed her back down and restrained her. Seth held her down by putting his hands over her breasts. She groaned in pain again, struggling even harder to get free, but the ropes just cut into her arms and legs more and more with every move she made.

Joshua and Lucas could do nothing but watch. Seth get on top of Venus and roughly fondle her. Venus barely moved and could only groan in agony.

Again, all Joshua and Lucas could do was watch and listen while they struggled to get free. Joshua looked away and tried even harder to get himself free.

Chapter 14

After what seemed like hours, the door suddenly creaked open again, and in came Segor with two other men.

Joshua and Lucas both had surprised looks on their faces upon seeing Segor.

Segor began to talk.

"I went back to that dung-eater's horrid cell, but apparently no one was killed there except the creature. I did, however, let the Minotaur out, so if they happen to cross his path, they most certainly won't make it," conveyed Segor, who didn't notice Joshua or Lucas in the corner.

Japeth looked at Segor and pointed towards the corner, showing Segor their catch. He also pointed out the girl on the bed.

"Ha, ha, ha! Thought you made it out alive, but I guess not," laughed Segor. "I bet you never thought you would see me again, huh? Ha, ha, ha! And what is this, an extra prize from the catch? Was she with them?" Segor asked, pointing to Venus.

"When we got them? Yes," explained Japeth.

"And we got them good, huh, boss?" smirked Seth.

"Yeah, yeah, real good," Segor said. "Well, I guess we can leave now. I see our little friend here is waking up." Segor walked over to the bed.

"Leave her alone!" shouted Joshua, tugging on his ropes.

Segor ignored his plea and said to Japeth, "What happened to her? Why are her clothes all torn?" Segor pulled her blouse up and over her partially naked body.

"Well, sir, we had a little bit of fun with her," replied Japeth.

"Meaning?" asked Segor as he lifted her back up and untied her arms from the bedposts.

"Meaning, we couldn't let her lay there on the bed and not use her…if you know what I mean," responded Japeth and chuckled.

"Yes, I know what you mean, Japeth. Come on. Knock that shit off. We have more important things to do." He shook his head.

Segor took Venus by the arm. Her blouse almost completely fell off of her, and her pants were torn up both legs. Obviously, she'd put up quite a fight, but after being drugged, she never had a chance.

"Gather everything together, and start carrying it out," Segor directed Japeth.

"Sure, boss, right away," answered Japeth. "Seth, you grab those swords and be careful. Gerrar, you take one side of the chest. Jerome, you take the other."

"Don't forget to leave our special package for those two, Japeth," Segor said as he dragged an almost-lifeless Venus out of the room. She struggled to stay on her feet.

"Right. I better get that now," replied Japeth.

He walked over behind the bed and came back dragging a burlap sack. The one end was tied with a rope, so he untied it and let the sack drop to the floor.

"What's in the sack?" Lucas asked of his captor.

"Ha, you think I am going to tell you and ruin the surprise? No way! Besides, you will find out soon enough. Have fun! This time you will *not* escape," replied Japeth.

It was several minutes after the group of renegades left that Lucas saw it! The burlap sack moved, and it was coming right for him! It was the largest thing he had ever seen! Its body was almost a foot in diameter, and it was only several feet away from him and Joshua! Both men tried frantically to free themselves, but they could barely move. The ropes were very tight. Neither man in this shape could fight off a creature like that! It was a giant python snake, probably fifty feet long—but the snake was not the only thing they had to deal with! Suddenly, they saw another tough and most deadly creature. There, coming at them from behind the bed, was not only the giant python but also a giant scorpion!

"Damn! Why is everything so fucking huge in this place," questioned Joshua. "How the hell are we supposed to get out of here?"

"I think that's the point. We're not," replied Lucas.

Joshua frantically searched for a way out of this predicament. He let out a loud grumble.

The giant scorpion made a quick jerk towards Joshua when it heard the loud noise.

"We have to get out of here and fast," whispered Joshua as he tried not to startle the scorpion again.

The scorpion held his ground as the snake slithered ever closer.

Joshua tried everything he could think of to break the ropes that held his hands behind his back, but it was no use.

"Agreed, but how," asked Lucas who also tried everything he could think of to get free.

"We have to get our hands free. Maybe you can reach my hands or I can reach yours. Let's try, you first."

Lucas lay down on the ground and tried to get as close to Joshua as he could. Then he reached for his hands behind his back. He could reach them!

The giant scorpion was only ten feet away, and the giant snake was crawling over Joshua's legs when Lucas finally freed Joshua's hands. Joshua quickly untied Lucas's hands and got ready to deal with the snake. Joshua reached out with lightning-fast hands and grabbed the snake's head. The body quickly coiled around his legs, but he went to work at killing the snake. Joshua, making sure not to put his hands on the poisonous fangs, reached into the mouth of the snake and pried its mouth apart. He used all of his strength to spread the snake's mouth open until he heard several loud snaps. Those were followed by several smaller crackling sounds. Blood squirted from the snake's mouth, and it started to release its hold on Joshua. A few seconds later, the snake's body went limp, and it stopped moving.

While all of this was going on, the scorpion stayed back, tail poised overhead, ready to strike.

Joshua tossed the snake aside and untied his feet just as Lucas freed himself. Both men quickly jumped to their feet and slowly inched towards the door, trying to avoid startling the giant scorpion.

"Wait," whispered Joshua. "Shouldn't we try and find our weapons and/or armor? In this condition, we are almost helpless."

"What about that giant scorpion?" asked Lucas, who checked to see if the scorpion had noticed them yet.

"We have time. It looks like he is busy with the snake. Quick, let's find some armor or at least a weapon or two."

As the scorpion poked and played with the dead snake, both men walked slowly over to the bed and peered behind it, looking for weapons or armor. They were in luck; behind the bed was their armor along with two long swords. They weren't their swords, but they would do for now. The rest of their possessions had been taken from them and were with Segor and his gang.

They quietly put on the armor and took the two long swords that were there and walked slowly towards the door. Just as they reached it, the giant scorpion let out a loud screech. Joshua and Lucas frantically pulled open the door and ran out into the corridor, slamming the door behind them!

Once they reached the outside corridor, they paused for a second to catch their breath.

"They only have a couple of minutes' head start on us," said Joshua, who led the way through a doorway in the lounge room after a couple seconds.

They both walked into the corridor and to the intersection with another corridor.

"I bet they went west in order to get out," stated Lucas.

"Yeah, I think you're right. Let's go that way. I want to get Venus back!" Joshua took off in the lead.

They walked through the corridor and secret doorway and back into the wine cellar. From there they marched through the chamber to the doorway that led to the steps. They went up the steps and through the long corridor outside the garden. When they got to the corridor with the deep gouges in the floor, they stopped and listened. They could hear faint noises coming from their right. It sounded like men talking and making a lot of noise, so they decided to find out who it was and went to the right, through the doorway and back into the barracks.

They proceeded through the doorway on the southwest corner and entered another corridor. Now they could hear the noises much clearer but still couldn't tell how far off they were.

Joshua and Lucas kept up a steady pace and walked into the chandelier room and back into the huge ballroom. The noises immediately got louder.

"We must only be a few yards behind them now," whispered Lucas.

"Sounds like it, doesn't it?" replied Joshua, who listened very intently for any sign of how close or how far away they really were.

"But now we have another problem," stated Lucas. He scratched his head and tried to listening very carefully.

"What is that?" asked Joshua.

"Which way did they go?"

"I don't know. We just listen at each doorway, and whichever one we hear the noises coming from, we go that way first," explained Joshua, who headed towards one of the archways.

"Okay. I'll go across on the other side, and you start right here," responded Lucas.

Lucas walked over to the other side and began listening at each archway for any noises. He didn't hear any! One after the other, nothing! Joshua got the same result. He heard nothing at any of the archways!

"How can that be? Nothing? That doesn't make any sense," stated Joshua.

Lucas returned to join Joshua.

"Anything?" he asked.

"No. Nothing. No noises anywhere. They just vanished."

"Same for me," Lucas responded.

"Damn, I was so sure they were right ahead of us," said Joshua as he looked around again.

"Well, either they left or went through the archway on the north wall," deducted Lucas, at a loss for any other solution.

"Let's not say they left. Besides, the door is locked," remembered Joshua.

"Okay, then let's try the archway on the north wall," directed Lucas.

"Works for me, Lucas. I hate to think they still have Venus with them. Who knows what they might do to her," said Joshua who remembered her bravery and great-looking body.

Chapter 15

S ilhouetted through a bedroom window, a woman brushed her hair with long, gentle strokes and stared out the window at some dogs running around the corral. The horses in the corral didn't seem to be bothered by the dogs frolicking. The silhouetted woman stood up and turned sideways. She slowly untied her nightgown straps, pulled the gown down off her shoulders, and let it fall down to the ground. From below the window, there came an unfamiliar sound, but she went about her business. She tilted her head backwards and shook her hair loose. Then she leaned over and let her hair fall in front of her. She ran her fingers through her hair and then down her sides. She stood there naked for a second or two and then walked over to the wardrobe. She pulled out a lace teddy and pulled it over her legs, past her hips, and then over her breasts. She tied the straps behind her neck and turned to get into bed. Suddenly, from outside her bedroom door was a sound as if someone was out there. She stopped, turned around, and walked slowly to the door. Just as she grabbed the handle, it burst open, and two men ran in and grabbed her. They threw her down onto the bed and held her down. She tried to scream but couldn't get one out before they gagged her. As she lay on the bed being tied up, one man began to search for something. He went over to the wardrobe and opened it up. Suddenly, three more men burst into the room. They drew their swords and attacked the two men already in the room. The man by the wardrobe went down with a gash to his back and sides. He slumped over into the wardrobe and bled ferociously. He quickly died!

The man holding the girl quickly drew his dagger and pressed it against her throat and crawled onto the bed next to her.

"Get away from me, or she dies," he screamed.

"Right," said one man as he pressed closer, waiting to see what the thief would do next.

"I mean it! She dies if you come any closer!"

The woman cried in pain, and a small trickle of blood ran down her throat.

"Better let her go, or we will kill you and her if we have to," stated one man. "There is no way we are letting you go tonight!"

"Please, let him go," moaned the woman.

She tried to struggle free, but the more she moved, the harder he pressed the dagger to her throat. She could feel it cut deeper into her skin.

One man turned to another and said, "You have a madman with a hostage. What do you do?"

The other turned to him and said, "Take out the hostage."

With those words, the first man threw his dagger into the left arm of the woman. She screamed in pain! The dagger cut her skin and banged into the wall behind her. She bent over in pain and was, for a split second, free from her captor. At that second, the other man threw a dagger that hit the thief square in the chest. He dropped his dagger and fell to the floor, grabbing his chest. The woman writhed in pain and screamed in shock at the turn of events.

"What the fuck were you guys doing?" she screamed and kicked at them.

"Just relax! We got you free, didn't we?" pointed out the second man, who went over to help her with her wound.

"Some knight in shining armor," she said.

"Grab that fucker, and take him to the jail. Another one down and another citizen safe for another night," stated the third man.

"Yeah, I'm real safe," the woman sarcastically replied.

"Really?" the man asked. "Would you rather we let him rape you like he was going to do, or do you think you might be able to handle a small cut on your arm?"

"Well, since you put it that way, I guess I am okay," she replied and covered the cut with some cloth she had by her bed.

"Okay, then. No thanks necessary," said the man. "We are out of here. Let's go."

The three men grabbed their prisoner and dragged him out of her room, out of the building, and down the road and out of view.

Joshua and Lucas went through the archway into a short corridor, which ended at a door. They listened, didn't hear anything, and then cautiously opened the door. Once it was open, they could see a chamber of white marble columns and ivory-tiled floors. In the north part of the chamber was a raised dais about four feet high. They carefully looked behind each column for their enemies but found none. They could see that upon the dais were two huge ornately carved thrones. There were also heavy purple draperies that reached from the ceiling to the floor. They walked onto the raised dais and searched the back of the draperies for any doors or clues.

Behind one of the draperies, which hung about a foot and a half away from the wall, were a couple of doors. Joshua opened one while Lucas opened the other.

"Nothing but an empty corridor behind this door," said Lucas.

"This one leads to another doorway," explained Joshua. "I'm going to see where it leads."

Joshua walked down the corridor to the door and opened it. Before him was another empty chamber. Disgusted at the dead end, he walked back to Lucas.

"There is only an empty chamber behind that door, too," described Joshua. "Damn it! Nothing! Now where do we go?"

Just as he spoke the words, they saw a dark figure come out of a hidden doorway to their left. Quickly, Joshua threw his sword at the figure. The sword flew through the air and hit the figure in the back. The figure dropped to the ground.

"Man, you are good with that thing," said Lucas, amazed at what he saw Joshua do.

"Looks like we did come the right way after all. We almost missed it, but you, mister," talking to Lucas and pointing at the fallen figure, "may have helped us save Venus's life."

Joshua disposed of the dead man's body in one of the empty chambers, and when the body hit the floor, it fell through a trap door in the floor. Joshua was surprised to see that. He was also relieved that he didn't go into the chamber—that could have been him falling through the trap door!

"Whew! Good thing we didn't go into that chamber," Lucas said after seeing what happened to the man's body.

"I'll say!"

Both men walked through the secret doorway and into a dead-end corridor.

"There has to be another secret passageway here somewhere. He wasn't here by himself," whispered Joshua.

He looked around for any indication that there was another secret doorway around.

They began pushing and pulling various parts of the wall. When they got to the southernmost part on the west wall, another hidden passageway popped open! They drew their swords and carefully peered in.

They could see a large chamber with a fireplace in it. There were four men in the chamber, milling about. Joshua and Lucas ran into the chamber, surprising the men and quickly attacking them!

Two of the men ran to the fireplace and banged on the back of it. A backdoor then opened, and out came a large creature. The two men ran forward again and attacked Joshua and Lucas.

The fight switched from good to bad for Joshua and Lucas. The final blow came when Joshua's sword broke in half. However, he was near the fireplace and reached up above the mantle and pulled down a sword that was hanging on it. He immediately felt magic surge through him, and he attacked again. He attacked with more power and precision than before.

The Ogre had stayed away until two of the four men went down, but now he advanced towards Lucas. Suddenly Lucas's sword broke, and he retreated. Lucas reached up and grabbed the last sword that was on the fireplace mantle. Acting like the sword drove him on, he immediately attacked ferociously at the Ogre. The Ogre never came close to Lucas before he went down. With a thunderous crash, the Ogre fell backwards to the floor and onto one of the chairs in the chamber. The chair was flattened! The battle began to swing into Joshua and Lucas's favor.

The sword continued to drive Lucas on, and he attacked one of the two remaining men. That man soon fell before Lucas or Joshua were even badly hurt. The last man called loudly for Segor and the others to remain where they were and for them not to come out and give themselves away. He then fell but not before he hit Joshua in the side and cut him. Joshua quickly bandaged it with a piece of cloth he found in the chamber and continued on. Lucas, after killing the final fighter, threw the sword down and held his hands together, shaking. Only at this time did Joshua really see what was in the chamber.

The chamber was a huge den filled with comfortable furniture and a large fireplace in a corner. There was a large plush couch, two comfortable chairs, one of which was crushed by the fallen Ogre, and a large table with four matching chairs. Lucas looked around and saw an aquarium in the room. There was a section of shelves on one wall that contained a number of figurines: a gold statue about one foot tall, an ivory elephant, several wooden carvings of various animals, a small jade statue of a man in a squatting position, and several miniature carvings such as a mahogany frog, an ebony fly, an ebony lizard, and a mahogany spider. There were also two decorated pewter plates propped up at the back of the shelf.

Joshua and Lucas found several books and tomes, all well-known literary works of the time; however, none seemed to have any real value to them. Then they examined the fireplace more carefully and saw the fireplace had a large mantle on it. Above the mantle was a large coat of arms mounted on the wall. It was carved of heavy wood and was colored gold with red bands crossing it at the top and bottom. A duck was depicted in the middle of the design.

Joshua remembered the bastard sword he had used and took a look at the scabbard it had been in. There were carvings on the hilt of the scabbard, but they seemed to be more ornate than rune-like.

Joshua, knowing his sword had some beneficial magical powers to it, took the scabbard to store his sword in. Lucas warned about his sword, saying it drove him wild with rage and made him attack wildly the nearest thing to him. Luckily, Lucas could get rid of it before it was too late for him or Joshua. The sword lay on the ground about twenty feet from where they were now.

"Don't use that one anymore," warned Joshua.

"Right," answered Lucas, still rubbing his hands.

Both men walked over to the back of the fireplace and examined the chamber that the Ogre came out of. They could see an area about twenty-five square feet behind the fireplace. There was nothing else in the chamber, so they left it. They also noticed on the fireplace several tools and a niche to the left that had wood scraps in it. They knew there was another chamber nearby because of the way the last fighter yelled to Segor and the rest to stay put. They checked the fireplace's niche, the table and chairs, the aquarium, and the plush couch again. They found nothing as to a clue where that chamber might be.

"Let's search the things on the shelves," directed Joshua.

"Good idea. I'll take the books and tomes; you search through the figurines."

"Fine," agreed Joshua, who walked over to the shelf and grabbed a book.

Each man took his time and searched through everything on the shelves as to any whereabouts of Segor and the rest, especially Venus. They had examined everything and found nothing unusual except the two pewter plates, so they took them down and found a small keyhole behind one.

"Damn! I betcha the key that fits that hole is the one I found in the wizard's laboratory, but they took that when they captured us," said Lucas. He searched for any other holes or a key.

"Well, all we can do now is wait. There is bound to be someone coming along this way again. It looks as though Segor has some sort of operation running in this castle, so one of his henchmen will be coming along shortly. Don't you think so?" asked Joshua.

"Yes, I suppose you are right. How long will we have to wait, though? I am getting really tired," said Lucas.

"I don't know, Lucas. Sorry you are getting tired, but they still have Venus, and I will not let them harm her again," stated Joshua, who wondered if they had already harmed her again or violated her like last night. He had a scowl on his face.

"Let's get rid of these dead bodies here, so it won't be so obvious that there were intruders here," said Lucas. He opened the secret passageway so that they could take the bodies, including the Ogre's, into the chamber with the pit in the floor.

With that gruesome task completed, they picked up the mess from the broken chair, placed everything back up on the shelf, and placed the swords back up on the mantle where they found them. Joshua, though, put one of the fighters' swords back up there instead of the magical bastard sword. Lucas, too, grabbed one of the fighters' swords to use as he had none at this time. With all of the preparations complete, they went into the hidden chamber and waited. They left the hidden chamber door open just enough so that they would be able to see out of it. They had a torch lit but finally decided to put it out after they made sure there was nothing in the chamber that would harm them.

Joshua decided to take the first watch so that Lucas could get some much-needed sleep. Hours went by, and nothing happened. Joshua woke Lucas up so that he could catch some shuteye. Again, nothing unusual happened during Lucas's watch.

Chapter 16

Long, golden rays of sunshine began to drench the countryside as a band of four men headed out of the town. Two men dragged large chests with them and started to fall behind the rest.

The sun was almost fully visible above the hilly countryside when the two reached an opening in a hillside. They pushed the vines and brushes aside and entered, dragging the chests with them. The others had gone on ahead and gone around the hill to another entryway.

The two men pulled the chests into the cave and rested for a moment.

"There has got to be a better way of doing this," stated the one man, wiping sweat from his brow. He sat down for a minute.

"Sure, but Segor said we had to put the stuff in here and not the regular storage chamber. Don't ask me why; he just said to do it this way," relayed the other man.

"Sure, anything for a little extra gold, huh?"

"I guess. Should we get going?"

"Yeah, let's go."

The men got up and continued to drag the chests further into the darkness of the cave. They soon disappeared from view.

Joshua and Lucas were both awake and waiting for something to happen, but so far, nothing and no one had entered the den. They quickly and quietly ate some breakfast rations and waited again.

Around midday, two men came through the secret door and into the den! They dragged two chests with them.

"Where the hell is everyone?" asked one of the men as he glanced towards the fireplace.

"I don't know," said another, "but it looks like they all left. What should we do now?"

"Well, now, I don't know what to do with this stuff we've got," he answered. "Let's just leave it and come back later." He glanced around the room.

The other man nodded in agreement, and the two walked back out of the secret doorway and left.

Joshua looked at Lucas and grimaced.

"Damn it! They left already," complained Joshua. "Now what do we do?"

"Just hold it. There have to be more coming. They were expecting someone to be here, remember?" cautioned Lucas.

"This is so frustrating, Lucas."

"I know, but patience, Joshua. Patience."

They got comfortable again and continued to wait.

When the two men got outside, one said to the other, "I noticed the secret doorway behind the fireplace was ajar. We have never left it ajar before. Besides, Jafar would have escaped if we had left it open, but I didn't see him. There must be something wrong."

"Must be someone or something in there," responded the other man.

"Maybe we should go and see who it is?" asked the first as he grabbed his sword and turned around to go back into the den.

"Right, just lead the way, Jessie," replied the second. He also grabbed his sword and followed Jessie back into the den.

Suddenly Jessie stopped!

"Wait, Jacob! I'll go in through the secret doorway behind the fireplace and see what's in there. You go back in and check the general's bedroom, okay?"

"All right. Then what?" asked Jacob.

"Well...give me twenty minutes or so to get around to the secret chamber, and then you enter the den again. If you hear me yell, quickly cover up the fireplace doorway with something heavy and then go tell Segor that there are intruders in the den. He'll know what to do next."

"Good plan, Jessie. Will do!" He patted his friend on the back.

Jessie turned and walked down the corridor and disappeared into a secret doorway.

Jacob gave Jessie about twenty minutes and then walked back into the den and slowly moved toward the fireplace. He stopped at the table and waited. It seemed like an eternity before he heard Jessie yell. He grabbed the table, turned it on end, and placed it in front of the fireplace's secret door. With the table in front of the door, he knew no one would be able to see out.

Joshua and Lucas had waited patiently for any sign of their enemy. Suddenly, a man came back into the den, one of the men who was there earlier. He had his sword drawn but laid it on the table and stood there. There was only one, not two, and they could sense something was up. They drew their swords and waited by the doorway, peering into the den. Suddenly, from behind them, out of the dark came a wild scream! Both men spun around and could see Jessie coming at them from out of nowhere! He attacked them. They both drew up their shields and attacked back. They had no trouble killing him but were very uneasy about the near calamity. They had no idea where he came from, and even after they lit a torch, there was no visible way that he could have gotten in. They even took a few seconds and searched for a secret passageway but found none.

"Whew," sighed Lucas. "That was way too close for me."

"I know it, Lucas. Where the hell did he come from?"

"I don't know. He wasn't here before."

"He must have come from a secret passageway somewhere, but I'll be damned if I can find it," stated Joshua.

Lucas and Joshua searched further for the doorway but could not find it!

"Well, he's dead. Let's just get out of here," said Lucas.

"Fuck, this is getting way too dangerous for us. This is a lot bigger than just a few men running around kidnapping Venus and stealing," declared Joshua.

Just then, Joshua noticed the fireplace door was blocked. He couldn't see out.

"Damn! The door is blocked and won't budge!" he yelled.

"Let's both try it," responded Lucas, who walked over to help Joshua with the door.

Jacob heard the small skirmish that went on behind the fireplace but ran over to the shelves anyway and banged on the wall three times, followed by two harder knocks and then four. The second section of the shelves opened up and revealed Segor. Jacob ran into the boudoir and saw Venus, Seth, Japeth, and Segor with two more men, Mosoch and Joseph.

"There are intruders in the den," explained Jacob, as Jessie had told him to do.

"So I hear from the commotion out there," said Segor. "Who are they?"

"I don't know ,sir. Jessie went around to the secret entryway to surprise them."

"Tell me how he found out about them. Weren't you just coming from a raid?"

"Yes we were ,but..."

Jacob proceeded to tell of how the two fighters noticed the doorway ajar and how Jessie had come up with the plan of attack.

Joshua and Lucas continued to try and open the door, but it was no use.

"There has to be a way out of here. We better find that secret doorway; we need help," said Lucas, who started tapping on the walls, floor, and ceiling in the fireplace chamber.

"Leave? Are you crazy? They still have Venus! We should have someone stay and guard the castle for anyone leaving," said Joshua. He feverishly tapped on the walls looking for the doorway.

"If we can get out of here, I'll go and get help and food. You can stay out in the ballroom or outside the castle for anyone leaving," responded Lucas.

"Okay, but hurry back, buddy. They still have my goddess!"

"We have to get out of here first. This is way bigger than we first thought. We aren't just dealing with Segor anymore. We need more help."

Just then, a portion of the wall nearest Lucas moved!

"I've found it!" exclaimed Lucas, pushing the door open.

Both men left the chamber and entered the throne room. From there, they proceeded back out to the castle entrance. On a hunch, Lucas tried the door.

"Look! The door isn't locked anymore," he said, finding the door rather easy to push open.

"Good, now get going and hurry back, Lucas," said Joshua as he looked for a place to hide until Lucas got back with help.

"Will you be all right here?"

"Yes, just leave a bit more food and get going. Hurry!"

"Alrighty then, I'm off! Don't do anything stupid like try to fight them all yourself. I know you, Joshua!"

"Just get going, I'll be okay, I promise."

"Okay, see you soon."

Lucas turned and started down the road towards town.

Joshua took up a position outside of the castle, a place where he could see anyone who entered or left the castle.

Chapter 17

Morning had broken, and a man entered the sheriff's office and closed the door behind him. Inside were four other men standing around a desk. One man seated behind the desk spoke to them.

"We have a big problem here. Joshua and I were on this adventure to find the Midas Orb for the town, but we have stumbled upon something a lot bigger than just the two of us can handle. Segor, the thief that we took with us on our journey, is the mastermind behind some crime ring," he said.

"Yes, we believe he runs the crime ring that is terrorizing our citizens here in Gnarda," replied one man. He puffed on a cigar.

"Well, then, we have a lot of work ahead of us. We have done pretty well as far as getting to the main headquarters located deep in the castle, but there are too many men for us to get rid of them for good."

Lucas got up and walked over to the office window and peered out.

"I know you don't want your women and children hurt anymore, so I am asking you men for a favor. I plan on returning to the castle, but we need your help. We want to rid the area of this crime and retrieve the Midas Orb for the town."

He turned back towards the group.

"Can we count on your help? Whatever you can do would be appreciated."

"Yes, I will help," responded one man named Abraham. "I will accompany you to the castle and help you get rid of these barbarians.

"Sure, I can help, too," replied another named James. "My girlfriend has already been raped by those thugs, and I'd do anything to get back at them. Count me in!"

James put his arm toward the center of the group in a united gesture. Abraham and then the two others followed suit and shook hands in the center of their circle, displaying unity.

"Fantastic!" exclaimed Lucas. "We leave in two hours. I need to get some supplies and rations first. Meet me back here in two hours, and be ready to go."

Lucas turned to leave the office.

"Oh, guys..." he paused. "Thank you."

"You're welcome, and thank you for helping us fight these bastards," replied another man named Simeon.

The fourth man in the group was Haran, a man of the law and the official town sheriff, at least until the real sheriff returned from a trip up the river to the town of Narthwood.

Joshua sat outside the castle watching for anyone to enter or leave, but no one did. He had waited for hours, but no one had come or gone. Finally, he could see down the road a small party of men riding horses and seemingly heading towards him. Several minutes later, Lucas and the others were upon Joshua and greeted him.

"Joshua, this is Abraham, Simeon, James, and Haran. They have agreed to help us out," stated Lucas as he got off of the horse and tied the bridle to a nearby tree.

"Great. Thanks, guys," welcomed Joshua, and shaking each one's hand.

"Thank you, Joshua, for helping the town with this severe problem of crime we have. You are to be commended for your loyalty to us," said Haran.

"Well, shall we get going?" Joshua said and walked into the castle.

They went into the great ballroom and from there went into the throne room.

"No one left while I was gone?" asked Lucas.

"Correct. No one left, and no one came in. At least, they didn't come through the front entrance," replied Joshua as he took the lead position in the party.

"Well, then, they must still be in here. Prepare for a good battle, guys. These men are armed and dangerous."

The party went into the secret passageway and proceeded into the den. Nothing had changed in the den, and they all went back into the secret chamber behind the fireplace and waited again. Joshua did notice that Jessie's body was now gone, but everything else seemed to be in order the way it was when they left just yesterday.

"Everyone, just relax and get ready. We could have company at any time," instructed Lucas.

"I sure hope they didn't hurt Venus," said Joshua pounding his right fist into his left hand.

"Don't worry. We'll get her out of here. All we need is another fighter to come in and get into the secret chamber. Then we can follow exactly what he does and get into the chamber, too," said Lucas who took a good spot to view the den.

The rest sat on the floor, ready to spring into action at a moment's notice.

Night had again fallen when she heard a creak from outside the door to her room.

Must be Gregory, she thought to herself.

She pulled the window shades shut and walked over to put her nightgown on. She took off her bra and panties and pulled her nightgown over her head and onto her body. She ran her fingers through her hair and shook her hair loose. The door handle moved! She walked back over to the bed and sat upon it. She couldn't wait for her husband to be with her again. It had been a long time since they'd made love. Tonight would be the night for a renewal of sorts.

The door started opening! She took a deep breath and stood up in anticipation.

Suddenly two men burst into the room and came right for her. Lily screamed! She turned to get away, but Kelvin grabbed her and pushed her face first onto the bed. Victor walked over to the bed and smiled. He held her down while she struggled to get free.

"What have we here? I hope we haven't kept you waiting," he said, running his hand down her back.

"Help!" she screamed.

"Cover her mouth! Do you want the whole town to know we are here?" demanded Victor.

"Sorry." Kelvin put his hand over her mouth and used his other arm to hold her down.

Lily kicked and wiggled around trying to get free, but the men were too much for her. She tried biting Kelvin, but he slapped her across the face when he felt her do so. She let out another scream.

"You had better not try that again, or you will not live to see another day. Think I'm kidding? Ask your man friend," said Kelvin.

"Let's see if we can find anything in here to make it worth our while," said Victor.

He searched the bedroom for anything of value while Kelvin held Lily down. Lily watched Victor tear through all of her personal things and take several brooches and pendants. He also found a small pouch belt with a gold ring inside.

"Whoa! We almost missed this one," he said as he held the ring up in the air to examine it.

"Let's do her and get out of here, Victor," responded Kelvin.

"Go ahead. I don't feel like it right now. I'll hold her for you."

Victor tied her feet to the bottom of the bed and held her arms above her head as Kelvin got on top of her and proceeded to rape her. Lily tried with all her might to get free, but the more she moved, the more it hurt ,and Kelvin's weight was too much for her.

After several minutes, he stopped and got off of her.

"You sure you don't want a go 'round? She ain't that bad," he said to Victor as he fondled her breasts.

"No, that's okay," he responded. "This is your turn."

Just as he said those words, from outside the bedroom came a loud sound! Kelvin jumped up and grabbed his sword. Victor headed for the door and paused as he heard a floorboard creak. There was someone right outside of the door! Victor grabbed his sword and held it above his head.

"Look out!" screamed Lily as she sat up to untie her feet.

Kelvin turned to go after her when the door burst open! Victor drove his sword downward! From the other side of the door came three men carrying swords. Victor hit the first, and he went down, but the other two quickly entered the room and attacked. Kelvin grabbed Lily as she screamed and held his sword under her neck. She was still naked but became very still, very quickly. The two other men killed Victor as the first man hit by Victor was lying on the floor, bleeding from the sword wound.

"Don't come near me, or she dies!" Kelvin held her tightly and pushed the sword up into her neck.

Lily screamed again!

"Okay, hold it," said the one man. "Let her go, and we will let you go."

"Yeah, right. I let her go and you two spear me like a shish kabob! I'm not stupid."

"Okay. What do you want?"

"I want my way out of here and free passage to wherever I want to go," demanded Kelvin. He pushed the sword harder against Lily's neck.

"Oww!" she screamed.

"Stop it, and you have a better chance of getting out of here. If you kill her, we definitely will kill you. Think about it," said one man.

The wounded man on the floor had stopped breathing. He was dead! Victor, too, had died from the sword wounds. From outside the window came another sound. It startled Kelvin. The two men saw their chance and darted for Lily and the man. Kelvin quickly recovered his composure and slashed Lily across the chest as he dropped her to the ground. He then turned the sword toward the two men. One of them, Marcus, had hit Kelvin in the side and turned to help Lily as the other one fought with Kelvin. Lily was bleeding from her chest, and Marcus quickly covered her up with a sheet from the bed. He carried her out of the room into the living room and put her on the couch. He ran to the door and called for help.

"Hey, Michael, get in here with some help. Lily has been hit!"

Marcus then ran back into the bedroom and arrived just as Kelvin drove his sword into Hareth's side. Hareth fell to the floor and moaned in agony. Marcus attacked Kelvin before he could recover from Hareth's murder. Marcus killed Kelvin with a couple blows to the body and turned to check on his friend. He was too late; he was gone.

When Marcus got back to Lily, Michael and two others were there attending to her.

"Get her to Doc's right away. I'm not sure how badly she was hit. I'm going to make sure everything is under control here and then meet you there."

"Okay, Marcus," replied Michael. He and the others picked up Lily and took her out of the house.

Marcus went back into the bedroom and checked on Farrell and then Hareth. Both men were dead, so Marcus went back into the living room and searched for anyone else. Behind the couch lay another body! Marcus checked to see if the man was still alive.

Gregory was dead!

After several hours, two men entered the den through the secret passageway. Lucas waited anxiously for them to open the other hidden door. The men were talking amongst themselves as they walked up to the shelves. One man knocked three times and then twice harder... Suddenly, from behind Lucas came a sneeze! It was Haran! The men stopped and reeled around, dropped their loot, and drew their swords.

"Let's go. Take them captive," whispered Lucas as he bolted for the doorway and into the den.

Haran, Abraham, and Joshua took out one of the two men with a full-force bull rush. Lucas, Simeon, and James were busy wrestling with the other man while Joshua and the others tied their man up. Lucas finally got the other man tied up and dragged him to the center of the den with the first.

"What are your names?" demanded Joshua, holding a sword at their throats.

The others had their swords drawn, ready to kill the two if they had to.

The first man spoke, "Our names are Riphath and Nahor, but that is irrelevant at this point."

"You don't know what is relevant or irrelevant to anything," said Joshua, disgusted with how things had turned out so far.

"How do you get into that secret room?" demanded Haran. "Tell us before we put you to death!"

"I would never tell you, even if you did put Nahor or me to death."

With those words, Haran flung his sword into Riphath's body and pulled it out again. Riphath screamed as the blood ran down his chest and onto the floor. Nahor, shaking, broke down.

"If you don't kill us, I will tell you how to get into the secret room, but don't kill me," he begged.

"Talk. Then we bargain," said Joshua. He grabbed Nahor by the hair and bent his head backwards.

"Okay!"

"No!" screamed Riphath. "Don't tell them, you idiot! Segor will have your head!"

"I will have your head if you don't tell us now!" screamed Joshua back at Riphath.

He then motioned to Haran.

"Enough of this! Do it!"

Haran stabbed Riphath again. This time Riphath slumped to the ground. He had blood gushing from his mouth and chest. He was dying! Nahor groaned in terror!

"Okay! Okay! Okay! I'll tell you! Don't kill me," he pleaded again. "You have to knock three times on the second section of the shelves, two more times, harder, and then..." He gulped. "You have to knock four times and wait for the door to open," explained Nahor still shaking and trembling from the sight of Haran's sword piercing Riphath's body.

Riphath's body jerked a bit and then lay completely motionless. Riphath was dead!

"If you are telling us a lie, don't expect to live very long," said Haran, who was ready to jab him with his sword.

"I, I'm... I'm not l-lying to you, I...I...I promise," stuttered Nahor.

Haran stayed back to guard Nahor while the others, with Joshua in front, stepped up to the shelves.

"The second section... Ready?" said Joshua.

He knocked three times and then twice harder. He paused and nodded to Haran, and then he knocked four more times. They waited.

When Haran saw the shelves start to come apart, he drove his sword into Nahor's chest and ran up behind the others. Nahor screamed!

"Segor, don't!" Nahor yelled with his last breath.

The shelves stopped halfway, but Joshua and Lucas could still see in. There was Segor!

Quickly, Joshua drove his sword into Segor's chest while the others filed into the chamber. Inside the chamber was Venus, tied to a bedpost, Jacob, Mosoch, Japeth, Joseph, and Seth.

Segor fell to the ground from Joshua's sword wound as the others entered the chamber and attacked. Joshua withdrew his sword from Segor's chest and raced over to Venus's side. Venus was tied up and awake but very weak. She had clothes on, but they were very loose and didn't cover much of her body.

Lucas took on Seth; James and Abraham took on Mosoch; Joseph and Simeon took on Jacob; and Haran took on Japeth. Joshua helped Venus out of the chamber. He carried her out of the chamber and put her in one of the chairs outside in the den. He told her to keep an eye on Nahor and went back in to help with the fight.

When he got back inside, there were three battles still going on. He saw Haran on the ground with a deep gash to his side, Mosoch on the ground with no head, and James helping Lucas with Seth. Joshua took on Japeth after Haran fell. Lucas and James were busy with Seth and overpowered him into submission. He surrendered to them. Simeon was not so lucky! He was badly beaten by Jacob and wound up dying before anyone could get over to help him. Jacob ran out of the chamber and into the den. Joshua left Japeth and followed Jacob into the den. Before he could reach Jacob, he had grabbed Venus. Venus screamed!

Jacob grabbed her and put his dagger under her neck!

"Stop! I'll kill her if you don't give up! Right now," yelled Jacob.

Venus screamed again!

"All right, all right," replied Joshua. "Just don't kill her!"

"Of course, if you kill her, you know we will kill you," responded Lucas.

Joshua and the others threw down their weapons and surrendered to save Venus's life. Japeth, Joseph, Jacob with Venus, and Seth surrounded Joshua, Lucas, Abraham, and James. Suddenly Nahor staggered to his feet and backed up Jacob's men. He had blood running down his chest, but he stood rather sure of himself.

Joseph and Japeth started gathering up the swords when Nahor fell over right on top of them! He was dead! Joshua saw his chance and plunged into Jacob, knocking him and Venus down. The dagger went flying backwards, and Joshua jumped on top of Jacob. In the brief instance that followed, there was a mad rush for weapons and bodies with James and Abraham throwing swords to all who didn't have any. Joshua grabbed his sword and pinned down Jacob underneath it.

"You stupid fool!" he yelled. "You shouldn't get any mercy from me, but I can't just kill you like this. You are going back to the town for proper punishment."

A huge battle followed. Joshua made sure Jacob was securely bound and gagged before checking on Venus, who was lying on the ground near the couch. He picked her up and laid her on the couch, trying to comfort her. She had blood coming from her elbow on her right arm.

Lucas fought with Seth, and Abraham and James fought with Japeth and Joseph while Joshua helped anyone who needed it. There was the constant sound of clashing metal and men yelling at each other until finally men started falling. The first to fall was Seth, who was vastly out-skilled by Lucas. Next to fall was Abraham, as Japeth had him out-skilled, but Lucas and James killed Joseph, and the tide turned towards good once again. Japeth went for Venus again, but Joshua hit him in the back with the broad side of his sword. Japeth turned and headed for the secret door! Joshua threw his sword, and it caught Japeth right in the back. Japeth fell, hitting the wall, and died soon afterwards. Joshua and Lucas had beaten the forces of evil once again!

With the battle over as quickly as it had started, Joshua, Venus, Lucas, and James headed outside with their prisoner Jacob.

Once outside, they mounted some horses that were tied up by some trees.

"We will take Jacob back to town for punishment and then come back here and finish what we started, okay?" asked Joshua, riding with Venus and holding her tightly to him.

"Sounds good to me. I need some rest though, so let's rest for the night and come back tomorrow morning," stated Lucas.

"Sounds great to me. I could use a night of sleep before going on."

They rode back to town mostly in silence, reflecting on their lost friends.

Chapter 18

"We are so glad you made it back alive," said one of the townspeople.

"I knew you would do it," said another.

"Hip, hip, hooray for Joshua and Lucas!" shouted another.

The small crowd that had gathered cheered!

"He is one of those murderers!" yelled one of the city people and pointed at Jacob.

"We figured as much. That is why we brought him back here for his just punishment. He is the only one who survived from the raiding party," explained Lucas.

He breathed heavily and tried to catch his breath from the long ride and battle that they just had.

"We will go back and get the stuff they robbed from the city as soon as we get some food and drink," finished Lucas, who got down from the horse and headed into the saloon.

He sat at a stool and said, "Give me a cold one, bartender."

Venus was in bed and trying to get some shuteye when there was a slight rapping on her door.

"Who is it?"

"It's me, Joshua, Venus. Can I come in?"

"Sure."

The door opened, and Joshua stuck his head around it.

"Are you decent?"

"Well, that depends what you have in mind, Joshua? I have a nightgown on if that is what you mean."

"Good. I mean, I'm glad you are doing okay," he said and closed the door behind him as he walked into her room.

Joshua walked over to her bed and sat upon it.

"How are you doing?" she asked him.

"Me?"

"Uh huh."

"I'm fine. No problems." He smiled and held up an "okay" sign with his fingers. "How are you?" he asked, more concerned with her than anything that might be wrong with him.

She smiled at him and touched his hand.

They held each other's hands for a while and just stared at each other.

"Well, I am glad you are doing well. I'll leave you to get some sleep tonight. I will be in the room right next to you, so if you need anything just let me know, okay?"

"Okay."

Again she smiled at him and kissed his hand.

He smiled back at her and got up to leave.

"If I need anything, I will come and get you," she reiterated.

"Yes, please do," he said and turned and left.

The door gentle closed, and Venus turned her head and closed her eyes.

"We'll see if he really means that," she whispered to herself and snuggled up to get some rest.

The cool night air glided into Venus's room, making her uncomfortable. She got up out of bed, walked out into the hall, and opened up Joshua's door. She peered in and was sure he was still asleep. She walked in, closed the door behind her, and walked over to his bed. She stood at the side of the bed for a moment and watched Joshua sleep. She pulled the covers off on one side of the bed and crawled in next to him. He stirred a bit but did not wake up. She covered them both up again and snuggled next to his warm body. She smiled and laid her head on his arm. There she dosed off to sleep.

For the first time in three months, the town had a restful sleep—no screams or new murders in the night. All of the livestock was still around in the morning, and most everybody got a full night's sleep.

Joshua opened his eyes and blinked. Was he dreaming again? He opened his eyes again and stared at her. Venus was lying next to him in his bed! He couldn't believe it! She looked so peaceful that he was careful not to wake her. He put his arms around her and pulled her closer and gave her a hug. She stirred a bit and wrapped her arms around him and hugged him back. He thought she was awake. He held her close for what seemed like an hour until she finally opened her eyes and smiled at him.

"Good morning. How do you feel this beautiful morning, Joshua?" she asked him and hugged him.

"I...I feel great. How about you?" he stuttered.

"I could not be better. I slept like a baby."

He pulled her tighter and hugged her again with his arms wrapped around her and crossed over her chest. She wrapped her arms around his and kissed his arm.

"When did you come in here?" he had to ask.

"Oh, I don't know, sometime early this morning. I was so cold in my own bed that I crawled in here with you. Is that okay?"

"Yes, that's fine. I was just wondering, that's all."

"You mean you don't mind that I was here with you?"

"No, not at all. Actually, now that I realize you are here, I kind of like it."

He kissed her head and hugged her again. Venus moved his arms just a bit and placed his hands over her breasts. Joshua smiled but didn't let Venus know how he felt. They lay there for a while and rested some more.

The townspeople supplied them with rations and drink for their journey and rounded up two more men to accompany them back to the castle to retrieve the town's belongings. Lucas, Joshua, Venus, Damascus, and Thare headed back out for the castle. It took them little over two hours to get back there, and they headed straight for the secret chamber. When they got there, Joshua noticed Segor's body was gone! His body was not to be found anywhere!

"Oh, oh," said Joshua after he realized the missing body. "Someone is still here! Be very careful, please. Venus, you stay with me!"

"Oh, yes, my master," she joked and put her head on his shoulder.

Joshua glared at her and then smiled.

Thare and Damascus did a little housecleaning. They piled up the dead bodies of the raiding party and put the bodies of the townspeople into the cart for a proper burial back in town. They took all of the figurines, pewter plates, books, tomes, and anything else they found that might have belonged to the townsfolk with them as they went back to town.

Joshua, Lucas, and Venus, now properly dressed in a blouse and denim pants and boots, searched the secret chamber where Segor had his headquarters. The chamber was lavishly furnished, including an intricately carved ebony bed, a similarly carved wardrobe, and a dry sink with a porcelain basin. Joshua noticed that in one corner of the boudoir stood two ceramic urns. One had a lid, and the other did not. When Joshua opened the urn, with the lid a spray of spores came out of it. The cloud completely engulfed Joshua, and he fell to the ground! Lucas and Venus were searching the bed and did not see what happened until they heard a thud. They both spun around to see Joshua lying on the ground and rushed to his aid. They couldn't see the cloud of spores and didn't know what happened to him.

"Joshua? Are you okay?" asked Venus, who shook him slightly to see if he would move.

"Joshua! What happened?" demanded Lucas. He propped Joshua's head up, so he could get some air.

After several minutes, Joshua finally stirred. Joshua slowly pushed himself into a sitting position and rubbed his head and tried to speak.

"Wh-wha-what happened?" he stuttered, rubbing his head again. "Where am I?"

"We don't know what happened. One moment you were by the urns, and the next you were lying on the ground passed out," explained Venus as she gently rubbed his forehead.

"Who am I?" he asked. "Who are you? Where am I?"

"You are Joshua. We are Venus and Lucas, your friends," pointed out Lucas as he helped Joshua to his feet.

Joshua sat upon the bed.

"Right. We are looking for the Midas Orb to help the people of Gnarda," explained Venus, who comforted Joshua as he sat on the bed.

She rubbed his forehead and eased him back onto a pillow.

"I don't remember any Midas Orb or how I got here. All I know is my head really hurts," said Joshua. "And you, young lady, are one fine thing." He winked at her while he tried to stand up.

"Yup, it's official," stated Venus. "You are still the same guy. That's for sure."

"You must have amnesia," explained Lucas. "Let's let him rest a minute or two. It may go away in a while."

"Good idea," said Venus and patted him on the back as they walked away.

They went over to where they found Joshua and looked for some reason behind his amnesia. Lucas cautiously opened an urn and peered into it. All he saw were dried flowers, nothing else. Then he opened and peered into the other urn. Inside he saw several silver balls. Lucas thought for a moment but realized they weren't the right size for the Midas Orb, so he left them there and closed the urn.

"I can't figure out what it was," explained Lucas to Venus. "There isn't anything around here that affected me the same way. I have no idea what happened."

"No matter," responded Venus. "He seems to be getting better, so it really doesn't matter anyway."

She looked back at Joshua, who gave her a wink. He had such a goofy look on his face, yet she couldn't help but crack a smile and look away, hoping he hadn't seen.

Joshua lay back onto the bed and closed his eyes.

Lucas walked over to the wardrobe. In a drawer at the bottom of the wardrobe, was a tray lined with velvet. In the tray's twelve compartments were the following: alkanet root, bitter aloe, asafetida, ash leaves, chamomile, catnip, gum camphor, blue flag, nutmeg, juniper berries, horseradish and china root. Also in the drawer was a small jewel case with a heavy gold-chain bracelet inside.

Lucas took the bracelet out of the case and held it up for Venus to see.

"Oh, it is so beautiful!" cried Venus. "May I have it?"

"I don't see why not. I'm sure not going to use it," said Lucas who tossed the bracelet to Venus.

Venus put it on. She looked very sexy with it on, but her clothes were wrong for her. She needed some better clothes. Her hair was a wavy, dirty blonde and was pushed away from her face. It looked like she had just brushed it, but she hadn't. Lucas thought for a moment about what she would look like wearing an evening gown—or a nightgown, for that matter. He smiled but continued on with his treasure hunt.

In a corner of the boudoir was a huge chest. Lucas cautiously opened it. Inside were five hundred platinum pieces and two gold rings. Venus wanted the rings, so Lucas gave them to her to wear. Lucas dragged the chest to the den for Thare and Damascus to take back to the town to share.

Minutes later, Damascus, Thare, and James came back into the den. Joshua awoke at the same time and remembered everything up to the last couple of hours.

"These five hundred platinum pieces are not part of the stuff taken from the townspeople. We have a list here, and there is no mention of five hundred platinum pieces being missing," explained Damascus. "Joshua, Lucas, it must be yours."

"Wow!" they exclaimed in unison.

"That is the most we have ever gotten in one journey, ever!" exclaimed Lucas, who graciously accepted the loot.

"Can you take it back to town for us?" asked Lucas.

"Sure, we should be able to do that for you," said Thare, who looked for a nod of agreement from Damascus.

He nodded in agreement.

"Besides, you did help us return the goods to the town. Thank you, guys," said Damascus.

He reached out and shook their hands.

"Thanks a lot to you, too," said Joshua when he shook Damascus's hand.

"Do you need someone to help you find the Midas Orb?"

"No, but thanks. I think we can manage now. We wouldn't want to put your life in danger, too."

"Good point," replied Damascus and laughed. "Alright then, take care and good luck, guys. You too, Venus!" He gave them a wave and turned and left.

"Yeah, goodbye!" said Thare as they walked out with the rest of the loot.

Chapter 19

Joshua, Lucas, and Venus walked back to the steps and down into the underground passageways. When they got to the east-west corridor, instead of going east like last time, they went west.

They went about seventy feet and then turned and headed south for thirty feet. They moved in another westward direction for forty feet, including a ten-foot descent down steps, and they entered another huge chamber.

The chamber had whips, chains, a rack, and other types of equipment commonly associated with bondage and torture. There was a huge, heavy chair with straps on the arms and legs situated by the north wall. There were heavy stocks on the south wall and a shallow pool of murky water in the center of the torture chamber. Directly above it, about twenty-five feet overhead, could be seen the end of a rope ladder dangling from an opening in the ceiling.

Lucas and Joshua went over to examine the chair just as Venus sat down in it.

"Hey, imagine what it must have been like to actually be put in here to die or to be tortured," she said.

Suddenly, a sliding panel of stone behind the chair opened.

"Stay back, Venus," warned Joshua, holding out his arms to protect her. "Lucas and I will check it out."

They drew their weapons and shields and slowly and cautiously entered a tunnel leading north. It sloped downward gradually until it split into two tunnels, one leading east and one west. All seemed to be okay, so they went back for Venus. Just as the guys reached opening back into the torture chamber, they heard a loud smack! They froze for a second!

They raised their swords and ran into the chamber!

Another loud crack!

Joshua froze when he saw the source of the loud noise.

"Venus, what in the world are you doing?" he asked. Joshua noticed she had one of the whips in her hands and was whipping the ground with it.

She looked over at him.

"Come here, big boy, get your just desserts," she said and slapped the ground again.

Smack!

"Hey, that isn't funny, Venus," he responded, backing up a bit.

"Why do you get such a kick out of this stuff, dear?" asked Lucas. He could see a huge smile on her face as she played with the whip.

"I was just always curious about the slave lords and the torture chambers of old Salem," she stated. "Didn't it ever interest you guys?"

"Nope. Can't say it did," responded Joshua.

"Not really, Venus. Let's get going," directed Lucas. He grabbed her by the arm and moved her along toward the passageway. He took the whip from her and threw it to the ground. "I feel safer now. Thank you!"

She winked at him as they left the torture chamber.

They all walked back into the passageway and down the sloping corridor.

When they got to the split in the corridor, Venus stopped as if sensing something wrong.

"Can you feel that?" she asked.

"Feel what, Venus?" asked Lucas, looking around and holding out his hand to feel anything out of the ordinary.

"I can feel heat. It seems to be coming from both tunnels," she reported as small beads of perspiration began to form on her forehead.

"Hey, so can I," said Lucas. He lifted his hands towards the east tunnel.

"Hmmm," said Joshua. "Better be careful. Not sure what that could mean."

They decided to go to the east. The tunnel snaked around until it entered a cavern. In the center was a lava pit. The lava was bubbling and steaming like a boiling cauldron. They could smell noxious sulfur fumes and saw where some of the steam seemed to exit through cracks in the roof of the cavern.

"I can't stand these fumes!" cried Lucas. "I gotta get out of here!" He had tears running down his cheeks.

"Then stay back. Venus and I will go on and see what we can find," said Joshua. She smiled back.

He started out along the edge of the pool of lava, followed closely by Venus.

"It looks like there is an opening on the other side," he said to Venus and grabbed her hand to help her along.

The heat was making both of them sweat, and Joshua noticed how Venus's skin began to glisten in the glow of the lava. He paused momentarily to wipe his brow before going on.

Lucas took up a position outside the cavern to guard against anyone trying to sneak up on them.

"Be very careful, you two," he warned as they disappeared out of sight.

"We will," replied Venus from the darkness beyond.

Joshua and Venus went through a tunnel in the north side of the cavern and walked down the winding tunnel, which eventually lead to a much smaller cavern. This cavern also had a pit in its center.

"I can't see anything down there," said Venus, who followed Joshua into the cavern.

"Here, I'll drop a torch down into it," said Joshua and he lit a torch.

He tossed it down into the pit. The small light disappeared from sight and made a slight crash sound when it hit the ground several seconds later. Just after the sound of the torch hitting the ground below, they heard snarls and growls come from the pit.

"I didn't see anything, but I sure heard something," said Venus, who pulled Joshua closer to her. She wrapped her arms around his chest.

"So did I," said Joshua, who tried to draw his sword just in case and held Venus with his other hand.

"Here, take out your rope, and lower me into the pit," Venus directed. "I'll take one of your swords and see what is down there. If there is anything down there that could harm me, you can pull back up."

Venus grabbed the rope and tied one end of the rope around her waist.

"I don't like it. You have no way to protect yourself while going down into the pit," said Joshua.

"I know, but there is no way I could pull you up from there, and I am light enough where, with one good yank, you could probably have me right out in a second's notice," she explained. She made sure the rope was secure and looked at him.

"I don't like it, but I guess it will have to do. Be very careful, Venus," warned Joshua, helping her over the edge of the pit.

"I will," she replied and reached up and kissed him on the cheek.

Joshua, startled by the kiss she gave him, tied the other end of the rope around his waist and slowly began to lower her into the pit. He had given her a torch and his sword before lowering her into the pit, but he could no longer see her, only the flickering torchlight in the darkness.

Lucas ventured back to the split in the tunnel and followed the other tunnel. He entered a cavern, much like the other one, with a lava pit in the center, bubbling ferociously. The sulfurous gases went up into the cracks above the pit. The glowing lava lit the whole cavern, and Lucas could see another tunnel leading further west. For some reason, these fumes weren't affecting him like the last ones, so he walked carefully along the edge of the pit and into the tunnel on the far side.

Lucas took the tiny, winding tunnel leading southwest into another cavern. On the far wall was a huge cloth covering a rather large, motionless, lumpy shape. Lucas drew his sword and thrust it into the cloth shape. The sword hit something hard, and the cloth tore! From within the cloth shape poured out several black balls, and they came right at him!

"Okay, lower me further," instructed Venus. She listened for any sign of the noises they heard earlier.

When she got about fifteen feet down, she heard the snarls and growls again but still couldn't see anything.

"I can hear the snarls again, but I don't see anything, Joshua!"

"Look along the surface of the pit wall," he instructed, holding her steady.

"Okay." She looked around. "I still don't see anything!"

Venus was just ready to call up to Joshua to let her down further when she spotted something out of the corner of her eye. She looked back with the torchlight and could see the source of the sounds. Her torchlight shone on a mouth-shaped figure right on the pit wall. She saw it snarl and growl and instantly knew it was behind all the sounds they had heard before.

"It is only a magic mouth, Joshua," said Venus. "You can let me down all the way now! I'll take a look around and see what's down here."

"Are you sure?" he called down to her.

"Yes, let me down farther," she responded.

"Be very careful, Venus," he said and lowered her farther.

Joshua let her down several more feet until she could touch the ground. She untied the rope from around her waist and began to search the inside of the pit for the Midas Orb. She found a pile of palm-sized black balls. There were about one dozen of them piled neatly in one corner of the pit.

"Joshua, I may have found the Orb, but I have to test these black balls first," Venus said as she picked up one of the balls.

"What? No, be very careful. Wait, I'm coming down there!"

Joshua quickly hammered a spike into the surface of the pit and tied his end of the rope around it. He had just finished tying the rope to the spike when a loud blast came from within the pit. Smoke and dust came shooting out of the pit, and he heard Venus scream! Then, as quick as it had happened, there was silence!

Amidst the cloud of dust and debris, he grabbed the rope and almost threw himself down the pit. When he reached the bottom, maybe ten feet down, he looked around but couldn't see Venus. Then he saw her huddled in a corner of the pit, opposite a pile of black balls. She lay motionless! Her blouse was torn and dangling from her waist. Her pants had also been ripped, and one leg completely showed through the denim pant leg. She had blood running down her right arm! Joshua ran to her and grabbed her into his arms.

She stirred.

"No, no," she said. "I'm all right. The ball just blew up when I scraped some of the paint off of it."

"Holy crap, I thought you were dead, Venus! Are you sure you are all right?" Joshua asked as he helped her to her feet. "You look pretty shaken up! And look at your clothes!"

"No. I'm all right," she said, standing by herself.

Only then did she realize she didn't have much in the way of clothing on. Venus looked up at Joshua, grinned, and shook the dust off her torn and tattered clothes.

"I have an extra cloak in my backpack, Venus. You can wear it," he said and opened his backpack to get the cloak.

"Thank you," she responded, putting the cloak on.

Joshua couldn't help himself and was staring at Venus as she dusted herself off and put on the cloak, covering her nearly naked body. He started to daydream...

Is she attracted to me as much as I am to her? Is this the way to the Orb? Am I starting to ramble on? Does anything I'm doing make any sense? Why am I really here? Will I get a chance with Venus? Would it be worth the time? When will we find the real Orb? How is Lucas doing? Is Venus her real name? How soft could her skin really be? Why am I asking myself these stupid questions? Is this all real or just a dream? Why do I have—

His dream was broken by Venus's voice.

"Joshua?" asked Venus, shaking him a bit.

"Yes," he muttered, not quite out of his trance yet.

"Are you okay? You seem to be in a daze," Venus asked and gently touched his face.

"Oh, yes, I'm okay. I was just thinking about some things," he reassured her and gently touched her back.

"Stand back by the wall while I test these balls. I don't want you getting hurt anymore." Joshua held his shield up in front of him to shield himself and Venus from any more exploding balls.

Using the tip of his sword, he scraped another black ball. Nothing happened! The black paint scraped off to reveal a basic stone ball. He picked up another one and did the same. Another stone ball! He tried a third ball. Still another stone ball!

"Looks like most of them are stone," said Joshua and picked up another and scraped the paint off of it.

Bang!

Dust and dirt flew everywhere. Joshua flew backwards right into Venus, knocking both of them to the ground. Venus landed on top of Joshua, both of them face to face. As the dust started to settle, Joshua noticed he was staring right into her eyes. He swore he could see right into her soul. Venus grabbed his cheeks in her hands and kissed him. Joshua gave in and relaxed for a moment. He grabbed Venus in his arms and held her tight. Her body was so light compared to what he was used to, and he enjoyed it. They lay there for a while kissing. Suddenly, Joshua stopped kissing her and reminded her why they were there and that

Lucas was waiting for them. Venus got up from on top of Joshua and pulled the cloak back up over her shoulders. Joshua got up and brushed himself off. He hugged Venus again and kissed her one more time. Then he picked up his shield, sword, and another ball.

"Stand back."

Bang!

The walls of the pit shook vigorously. Again Joshua went flying backwards and into Venus! They both hit the ground again. This time Joshua bounced right back up and grabbed another ball. Venus, however, stayed on the ground. She didn't move! The cloak had been blown off her, and her nearly naked body lay on the ground motionless! Joshua was getting mad and quickly scraped another ball. It was a stone ball. He threw it aside and picked up another one. By chance, he glanced back at Venus and saw that she wasn't moving. He threw the ball down and went to her aide. When the ball hit the ground, it exploded, once again the blast throwing Joshua into Venus. Joshua and Venus lay there for several minutes in a heap. Neither one moved! Finally, Joshua stirred and rolled off of Venus. She was still breathing, but she didn't move. Joshua leaned over her to check her breathing, and when he did so, she kissed him. She smiled and Joshua sighed in relief.

"Aw, damn, I thought you were dead, Venus," he said, sighing in relief.

"Too bad, Joshua. I'm still here," she said and smiled again.

"Too bad? What do you mean, too bad?" he asked. He helped her sit upright.

"Well, I am still here. You won't be that fun-loving, do-every-girl-you-can bachelor anymore. I'm back." She smiled again.

"Yeah, whatever! Are you all right?" Joshua asked.

"Yes, just let me rest a while. It gets pretty tiring having you falling all over me all the time," she joked and giggled.

"Ha, ha. Okay. That will be enough of that," he replied and started to get to his feet.

She reached up and grabbed him. She pulled him towards her, and he lost his balance and fell onto her again. She wrapped her arms around him and kissed him. Again they lay there and kissed for what seemed like minutes. Joshua loved it when Venus, this time, suddenly stopped kissing him and reminded him why they were there.

"Well, you pulled me on top of you, remember?" he said as he got up.

"Well, I know a good thing when I see it," she said and also got to her feet.

Again, she brushed the dust and dirt off her nearly naked body and picked up the cloak and pulled it back over her shoulders to cover herself again.

Joshua picked up one of the remaining four balls and tried it. Another stone ball! And another stone ball was thrown aside!

"Two to go! What are the chances one of them is the Midas Orb?" he asked.

"Fifty-fifty?" Venus asked and picked one up. "Here, try this one. It feels good to me." She handed him the ball.

"Get behind me, and cover your eyes."

"All set," she responded, holding onto his waist.

Lucas turned and ran as fast as he could but was hit in the back by one of the tumbling balls. He got tripped up and fell to the ground, sprawling. The balls rolled to the far corner of the cavern and stopped against the walls. Lucas got up very gingerly and looked around. He still remembered where he was but was a little shaky. Lucas looked through the balls. They were all black balls about the size of cannon balls. He carefully scraped ball after ball, checking to see if any of them were the golden Midas Orb. None were. After all of the balls were checked, he searched elsewhere, but there was nothing else in the cavern, so he exited and went back to the first lava cavern. He took up a post outside of the cavern and waited for Joshua and Venus to come back.

Joshua took the ball and laid it on the ground in front of them. He took his sword, raised his shield, and scraped the paint. The paint scraped off to reveal a gold ball. The Midas Orb!

Joshua couldn't believe it. He turned around and looked at Venus. Her mouth was open in amazement.

"How did you know?" he asked.

"Woman's intuition, I guess." Venus ran up and hugged Joshua.

He grabbed her and spun her around and then kissed her again.

They both stood there staring at the Orb. They couldn't believe it! It was really true!

Joshua picked up the Orb and peeled the rest of the paint off of it. He held it up for them to look at and it seemed to glisten in the torch light. He put it in his shoulder sack and hugged and kissed Venus again.

"I'm very proud of you," she said.

"Well, thank you," said Joshua and started to blush. "You were very good, too!"

"Oh, you haven't seen me when I am good, Joshua," she said with a smirk on her face. "But you will, just you wait!" She patted him on the back. "When I'm good, I'm good, but when I'm bad, I'm better." Again she smirked at him and winked.

Joshua smiled back and then gathered their belongings that had been strewn all over the cavern. They both headed back up the rope. Venus went first and then Joshua. When they reached the top, they gathered up the rope and went back out to find Lucas.

Chapter 20

Lucas stood there for what seemed like hours.

"I hope they are all right," Lucas said to himself as he started to pace.

Lucas was propped up against the cavern wall waiting for Joshua and Venus to return when he heard noises from deep in the cavern.

He went into the cavern and could see Venus and Joshua come out from the far tunnel. A cloak hung loosely over Venus's nearly naked body. Lucas noticed several bruises on her sweaty, dirty body. He also saw blood along her right arm and saw that Joshua was dirty and ragged-looking as well. Lucas had a worried look on his face.

"What happened to you two?" he said and pointed out the dirty clothes on Joshua and the way Venus stood there nearly naked.

"Well, Lucas, old chap," started Joshua. He was smiling and walking with his arm over Venus's shoulders.

Lucas started his story first. "I went searching for the Midas Orb down the other tunnel, but I didn't find it," he said.

"Lucas, you will never guess what we did," Joshua continued.

"I don't think I even want to know, do I?" Lucas responded and turned away to avoid staring at Venus's body. Her sweaty, dirty body was glistening in the light from the hot lava, and she wore a huge smile on her face.

"Oh, Lucas, you'd be so happy to know what we know," said Venus, who came over to him and gave him a kiss on the cheek and a big hug.

Lucas felt her press her body against his and smiled back at her, giving her a hug back.

"Really?" he asked after the hug. He was a bit embarrassed.

He glanced over at Joshua to catch a reaction from him. Joshua was getting something out of his shoulder sack.

"We found the Midas Orb!" Joshua pulled it out of his shoulder sack and showed it to Lucas.

"Wow, holy cow!" exclaimed Lucas. "I had almost given up hope of ever finding that thing."

"Well, we didn't. Did we, Joshua?" asked Venus, grabbing him by the arm and hugging him.

"Nope, not us," answered Joshua, who smiled back at her and hugged her back.

"If I may ask, Venus," Lucas asked, "what happened to you? Didn't you start this journey with clothes?" He was dying to know the details even though he didn't want to ask Joshua for any.

"Yes, I did. But you see," started Venus. She pulled the cloak over herself. "There were several exploding balls down there, and every time we found one, more of my clothes were torn off." She looked at Joshua and started to laugh. After seeing her laugh, he, too, began to laugh.

"Actually, it is a long, interesting story. I will tell it to you someday, Lucas," replied Joshua.

"Okay, I knew I shouldn't have asked, but thanks for staying safe and making it out alive," Lucas said and hugged them both.

They walked out of the caverns and back into the torture chamber with large smiles on their faces. Their smiles quickly disappeared when they saw what was waiting for them!

The wizard Wthai was standing in the torture chamber!

"It's the general's wizard," said Venus and grabbed Joshua's arm and held on tight.

Wthai was readying a spell when Joshua and Lucas darted after him. He got his spell off and was narrowly missed by Joshua, who had thrown himself at Wthai and by Lucas, who had hurled himself into Wthai. The spell hit Joshua dead center, taking him to the ground.

Joshua was hit with a magic missile spell! Lucas went flying into Wthai and missed getting hit by the spell. Venus, seeing what had happened, quickly ran up to Joshua and helped him up. She took off the cloak, threw it aside, and ran naked, towards the wizard. She flew at him with a flying drop kick. She hit her mark dead center! The wizard fell flat to the ground, knocked out! She bound and gagged him with rope that Lucas threw to her. Venus had beat the mad wizard even before he had a chance.

Lucas got up, grabbed Venus's cloak, and walked over to her. She put the cloak on and hugged him. They went over and picked up Joshua and made sure everyone was okay and then went over to Wthai. They stood him up and pushed him out in front of them and started to walk out of the torture chamber.

"Pretty stupid, old man," stated Joshua. "Why don't you just relax and do as we say, okay?"

The wizard said nothing.

"Good thing you moved so fast, Venus. Thanks," congratulated Lucas.

"No problem. You guys have helped me out enough, so I figured I may as well help you out once." She smiled at him and patted him on the back.

They headed back to the wine cellar, up the steps, and through the barracks, where an Ogre met them!

"Wthai, you had better get him out of our way, or we will kill you and the Ogre," threatened Joshua, who put his sword under Wthai's neck.

Wthai prepared a spell, and it went off. It hit the Ogre but didn't kill him. The Ogre turned and ran out of the chamber and down the corridor.

"Good, Wthai," said Venus and patted him on the back and then pushed him along.

The group proceeded on through the chandelier room and then into the great ballroom. Thare and Damascus, who were taking down the tapestries of the knights doing heroic deeds, met them.

"Well, howdy," greeted Joshua, Lucas, and Venus.

"We have found the Midas Orb! Our job is done," stated Lucas.

"Congratulations," said Thare and came over and shook their hands. Damascus followed and also congratulated them.

"What are you guys doing back here?" he asked.

"Well, we thought we would take everything of value out of here and then let it sit and decay," said Damascus who pulled down a tapestry.

"Well, we are done here. Take whatever you want," said Lucas. "Wthai here says so! Don't you, Wthai?"

Wthai nodded his head in agreement with Lucas. Wthai had a dejected look upon his face at seeing his castle being destroyed.

"So, you have captured the mad wizard, too! Well, well," said Thare as he turned to take a tapestry out to the cart. "You've had a busy time of it."

"Wait a minute, and we'll take you to Gnarda on the horses," said Damascus, who walked some more things out of the castle.

"Thanks," they all said in unison.

Damascus and Thare drove the cart while Joshua, Venus, and Lucas rode with the cargo in the back. It took about two hours to get back to town. Joshua and Venus took the two hours to get to know each other better. Lucas sat silently, remembering everything that had happened to them on their journey. Suddenly, he remembered that Segor's body was gone and had not been found!

Wonder what happened to Segor? he thought to himself as he watched the miles go by. Every now and then, he would glance over and see Joshua and Venus kissing each other.

I wonder if they will get married? Will I ever find someone like that? Does this cart get bumpier as we go along or is that just me? When will I be famous? How many miles is it exactly from the castle to town? Why am I really here? Is it really over? How many stars are there in the sky? Are the nights getting colder yet? How old is Venus? Is that really her name? Should I stay in Gnarda or return home? Maybe I should stay and try for Venus myself...

No! he thought to himself. *They make a great-looking couple. She obviously likes him, and I know he likes her. Geez, quit all of this thinking. You're going to go mad, Lucas!*

Several hours later, they were in front of the new general and leader of Gnarda, presenting the Midas Orb to him. The people of Gnarda were most thankful and threw Joshua and Lucas a huge festival to thank them for their services.

At the celebration, Joshua had some time to make a little speech. "People of Gnarda," started Joshua, "today we have returned to the town what was rightfully yours!"

The crowd cheered!

"We return the Midas Orb in all of its glory back to the people of Gnarda," continued Joshua, giving the orb to the leader of Gnarda, General Mahoney.

The crowd cheered again!

Joshua stepped aside, and General Mahoney took the orb and spoke. "The people of Gnarda and I would like to thank both you and Lucas, Joshua, for a job well done. We would also like to say thank you to our forgotten sister, Venus, for her help in this matter."

The crowd cheered again!

"We would like to make you honorary citizens of the town. You are welcome back here to visit anytime you want," finished the general. He shook hands and hugged each member of the victorious party.

The crowd cheered again!

"Now," stated the general, "let the festival begin in honor of our newfound friends!"

The crowd cheered and carried Joshua, Lucas, and Venus off on their shoulders. The festival was held in the town square and contained a banquet and bonfire. Many different foods and drinks were offered, and hundreds of townsfolk individually thanked the men for their gift back to the town.

Chapter 21

About one year later

About one hundred people had gathered in the temple. There was standing room only as they all awaited the bride. From the rear of the temple came Joshua and Lucas up the aisle. They were followed by two other men, Damascus and James, and then three very beautiful women, Jodee, Heather, and Esther. Suddenly, the music stopped, and the flutist began to play. From behind a door in the back of the temple came a beautiful woman dressed in white, carrying the biggest bouquet of flowers ever. She slowly made her way up the aisle and joined Joshua at the altar. The Druidanis priest came forth and greeted everyone.

"Welcome to this festive day," he began. "We are all joined here today to witness the union of two souls, lost for years, now to be joined together as one. Let us begin. Please sit down."

The crowd sat.

"Joshua, you have come to me today to take Venus as your beloved wife," continued the pastor. "And, Venus, you have come to me today to take Joshua as your beloved husband."

"Yes," they both responded in unison.

"Then, Joshua, repeat after me. I, Joshua, do hereby take thee, Venus, to be my beloved wife."

He repeated the words exactly.

The priest continued, "In disease and good health, in richness and poverty, until the end of my days."

Joshua finished.

"Now, Venus, repeat after me." The priest said the words again for Venus to say her vows.

Venus repeated the words exactly.

The priest turned towards the crowd.

"By the power given to me by the temple of Druidanis, I now pronounce you husband and wife. Joshua, you may kiss your lovely wife."

Joshua leaned over and kissed her.

The crowd cheered.

"This ends the celebration of marriage between Joshua and Venus. What we have put together, let no evil take apart. Go and find love in each other." The priest finished and backed up, putting Joshua and Venus front and center.

Joshua and Venus turned toward the crowd and, arm in arm, walked out of the temple.

As the temple emptied, one cloaked figure, strangely close to the back of the temple, walked up and whispered something to the priest. The priest nodded and then held out his hand. The figure placed a small sack into his outreached hands and disappeared through the side entrance to the temple.

Several Months Later

*N*ight had already fallen, and through a window could be seen the silhouette of a woman. She turned and pulled down the shade and then walked over to the wardrobe. She took off her undergarments and pulled her nightgown over her head and onto her body. She ran her fingers through her hair and shook her hair loose. She went over to the dresser and picked up a brush and brushed it through her hair several times. Then she walked over and sat upon the bed. Suddenly, she stood up and dropped the nightgown off her shoulders. She stood there completely naked, waiting. From the doorway came two figures. The woman quickly scrambled for her nightgown and screamed. She scrambled to get away. The two figures threw the woman back onto the bed and could be seen standing over the bed, struggling with her. A lengthy struggle ensued, and the figures disappeared from view.

In another room of the house was a body lying on the floor. Blood surrounded the body, and it appeared lifeless... It was the body of James!